My Secret Unicorn

Stronger Than Magic
and
A Special Friend

Two exciting adventures in the
My Secret Unicorn series
together in one bumper book!

★

Have you ever longed for a pony? Lauren
Foster has. When her family moves to the
country, her wish finally comes true. And
Lauren's pony t⸱⸱⸱⸱⸱⸱⸱⸱⸱⸱⸱ more
special than

D0813131

Other Books in the My Secret Unicorn *series*

My Secret Unicorn

Stronger Than Magic
and
A Special Friend

Linda Chapman

Illustrated by Biz Hull

PUFFIN

PENGUIN BOOKS

Published by the Penguin Group

Penguin Books Ltd, 80 Strand, London WC2R ORL, England

Penguin Group (USA) Inc., 375 Hudson Street, New York, New York 10014, USA

Penguin Group (Canada), 90 Eglinton Avenue East, Suite 700, Toronto, Ontario, Canada M4P 2Y3
(a division of Pearson Penguin Canada Inc.)

Penguin Ireland, 25 St Stephen's Green, Dublin 2, Ireland (a division of Penguin Books Ltd)

Penguin Group (Australia), 250 Camberwell Road, Camberwell, Victoria 3124, Australia
(a division of Pearson Australia Group Pty Ltd)

Penguin Books India Pvt Ltd, 11 Community Centre, Panchsheel Park, New Delhi – 110 017, India

Penguin Group (NZ), cnr Airborne and Rosedale Roads, Albany, Auckland 1310, New Zealand
(a division of Pearson New Zealand Ltd)

Penguin Books (South Africa) (Pty) Ltd, 24 Sturdee Avenue, Rosebank, Johannesburg 2196, South Africa

Penguin Books Ltd, Registered Offices: 80 Strand, London WC2R ORL, England

www.penguin.com

My Secret Unicorn: Stronger Than Magic first published 2003
My Secret Unicorn: A Special Friend first published 2003
First published in one volume 2006

2

Text copyright © Working Partners Ltd, 2003
Illustrations copyright © Biz Hull, 2003
Created by Working Partners Ltd, London W6 0QT
All rights reserved

The moral right of the author and illustrator has been asserted

Set in 14.25/21.5pt Bembo

Made and printed in England by Clays Ltd, St Ives plc

British Library Cataloguing in Publication Data
A CIP catalogue record for this book is available from the British Library

ISBN-13: 978-0-141-32120-2
ISBN-10: 0-141-32120-2

My Secret Unicorn

Stronger Than Magic

As Lauren reached the
paddock, she saw Twilight still
lying where she had left him. His nose
was resting heavily on the ground, his eyes
were closed . . . 'Twilight!' she gasped. 'What's
the matter? You look really ill!'

For Bramble – my own Buddy
– you loved life so much.
I miss you every single day.

CHAPTER
One

'I love this place,' Lauren Foster whispered as she sat on Twilight's warm back. Fireflies danced around them, lighting up the dusky shadows of the peaceful forest glade.

Moonlight shone on Twilight's silvery horn as he nodded. 'Me too.'

Lauren patted him. She could hardly believe how lucky she was. Most of the time, Twilight looked like any ordinary grey pony, but when she said the words of the Turning Spell, he transformed into a magical unicorn and they flew to places like this secret glade in the woods.

'When we're here, I feel like anything could happen,' Lauren said, looking round at the unusual pinky-grey rocks.

'That's because it's a special place,' Twilight told her. 'There's magic in the air.' He snorted softly. 'Shall we stay here or shall we fly some more?'

Lauren glanced at her watch. 'We should really go home.'

Lauren's parents had no idea that Twilight was a unicorn. At the moment,

they just thought she was outside in his
paddock, feeding him.

'I could use my unicorn powers to see
whether they're worrying,' Twilight
suggested. 'If they aren't, we could stay
out a little longer.'

'That's a great idea,' Lauren replied.

Twilight trotted over to one of the unusual rocks at the side of the clearing. As a unicorn, he had many magical powers. One of them allowed him to use the rocks of rose quartz to see what was happening anywhere else in the world. Touching his horn to the surface of one, he said, 'Granger's Farm!'

There was a bright purple flash and mist started to swirl. As it cleared, an image of Lauren's home – Granger's Farm – appeared in the rock. Lauren slid off Twilight's back to look more closely. She could see Twilight's paddock, the surrounding fields filled with cows, her bedroom window, her mum's car . . .

'Lauren's mum and dad,' Twilight said to the rock.

The picture wobbled and suddenly Mr and Mrs Foster appeared. They were talking, but all Lauren could hear was a faint buzz. Tucking her long, fair hair behind her ears, she leaned closer to the rock. The buzz turned into voices.

'Is Lauren still outside with Twilight?' she heard her dad say.

Lauren tensed, but to her relief her mum spoke calmly.

'She is, but don't worry. She knows to be in by bedtime. She just likes spending as much time with him as possible,' Mrs Foster said, smiling. 'It's one of the best things about having moved to the country. Lauren and Max can have so much more freedom. If we were still in the city ...'

Lauren saw her dad take her mum's hand. 'Moving here was the best thing we ever did,' he said.

Lauren sat back on her heels. 'It's OK,' she said to Twilight. 'I think we're safe for a while.'

'Shall we do some flying then?' Twilight said eagerly.

'In a minute,' Lauren said. She was enjoying looking at her family. 'Can I have a look at Max first?'

'All right,' Twilight said obligingly. 'Max!' he said.

The picture focused to show Max,

Lauren's six-year-old brother. He was
playing in his bedroom with his Bernese
mountain dog puppy, Buddy.

Lauren could tell from the way he was
holding a dog treat in his hand that he
was trying to get Buddy to sit.

She grinned at Twilight. 'Max and Buddy are starting dog-training classes tomorrow.' She watched the picture for a few more seconds. It was fun not being seen. 'Let's have a look at Mel now,' she said to Twilight. 'Just quickly.'

Mel Cassidy was Lauren's neighbour and one of her best friends. Twilight murmured Mel's name and the picture changed to show Mel sitting in her bedroom with her mum. Mrs Cassidy had her arm round Mel's shoulders.

'Mel's crying!' Lauren said in alarm. She started to lean forward and then stopped. Listening to her own family was one thing, but somehow listening in on a friend talking to her mum didn't seem right. 'I don't know if we should listen,' she said doubtfully.

'But perhaps if we know what's wrong, we can help,' Twilight pointed out.

Lauren hesitated for a moment. She and Twilight were good at helping people in trouble. That's why unicorns came to live in the human world – to use their magical powers to do good deeds with their human owners. She looked at the picture in the rock. Mel looked really upset. Quickly, Lauren made up her mind. 'OK, but we'll only listen for a second,' she said.

Lauren and Twilight leaned closer.

'It's not fair,' she heard Mel say. 'I just can't do it, Mum. I've asked Mr Noland to explain twice now and I still don't get it!'

'You'll just have to ask Mr Noland to go through it again,' Mrs Cassidy said gently.

Lauren frowned in surprise. Mr Noland was their class teacher. What could be upsetting Mel?

'But then Lauren and Jessica will think I'm really dumb!' Mel cried.

'I'm sure they won't,' Mrs Cassidy said, hugging her. 'They're your friends.'

'But they can do fractions. It's just me who can't!' Mel said.

Fractions! Lauren sat back and the voices faded to a buzz again.

'Fractions?' Twilight said, sounding puzzled. 'What are they?'

'They're something we're doing
in maths,' Lauren answered.

'So it's nothing serious then,' Twilight
said in relief.

'Well, I don't know.' Lauren hesitated.
'If Mel's upset by it, then it is serious.
She seems to think Jessica and I will
laugh at her.' She shook her head. 'But
we'd never do that. We don't care if
she can do fractions or not. She's our
friend.' She chewed a fingernail. 'Poor
Mel,' she said softly. 'I wish I could help
her.'

Twilight looked doubtful. 'I don't think
any of my magic powers can help people
do maths.'

'I guess not,' Lauren said. 'It looks like

this is one problem I'll have to solve on my own.'

Twilight touched his horn to the rock. With a purple flash the picture disappeared. 'Let's go flying now,' he said.

Lauren didn't need any more encouragement. She vaulted on to Twilight's warm back. Taking two strides, he leapt upwards into the sky.

The wind whipped against Lauren's face and her hair blew out behind her as they swooped through the air before finally flying back to Granger's Farm.

'So, how are you going to help Mel?' Twilight asked her as they landed.

'I'm not sure yet,' Lauren replied. 'But I'll try to think of something by tomorrow.' She hugged him and said the Undoing Spell.

There was a purple flash and suddenly Twilight was no longer a unicorn but a small grey pony.

'Good night, Twilight,' Lauren whispered.

Twilight whickered softly and, giving him one last hug, Lauren hurried into the house.

Two

'Lauren! You're going to be late for school!' Mrs Foster called up the stairs the next morning.

Lauren pulled a brush through her hair and hurried downstairs. School mornings were always a rush. As she ran into the kitchen, she almost fell over Buddy.

'Sit, Buddy! Buddy, sit!' Max was saying.

Seeing Lauren, Buddy leapt up in delight. Lauren tickled his ears. 'Hey, boy,' she said.

'Buddy! Come here and sit!' Max commanded sternly as the puppy gambolled around Lauren's legs.

Buddy crouched down with his front legs and stuck his bottom playfully in the air. 'Woof!' he barked, before bounding off wildly around the kitchen.

'He's going to be just great at obedience classes, Max,' Lauren teased as Buddy skidded to a halt too late and cannoned into the fridge door. 'He'll be bottom of the class.'

'He won't!' Max cried. 'Mum!' He turned to their mum. 'He won't, will he?'

'Buddy will be just fine, honey,' Mrs Foster said reassuringly. 'Lauren, stop teasing Max and eat some breakfast.'

Lauren sat down and buttered a piece of toast. Max was trying to open a new jar of chocolate spread.

'Come on, Max,' Lauren said impatiently. 'We'll be late.'

Max twisted with all his strength but the lid wouldn't come off.

'Here, let me,' Lauren said, taking it from him and opening it in one go.

'Lauren!' Max protested. 'I wanted to do it! You always interfere!'

'We'd have been here all morning,' Lauren told him.

'That's enough, both of you!' Mrs Foster said, running a hand through her hair. 'Finish your toast and let's go.'

'Hi, Lauren!' Jessica Parker called as Lauren ran into the classroom just before the bell rang.

'Hi,' Lauren said. She still hadn't thought of a plan to help Mel and it was troubling her.

'Samantha and I were looking at ponies for sale in a magazine last night,' Jessica told Lauren. 'There were three that we liked the sound of. We've been trying to get Dad to ring up about them.'

'Any luck?' Lauren asked. She knew how desperate Jessica and her stepsister were to have a pony.

Jessica sighed. 'No. Dad says we've got to wait until the summer holidays.'

Just then, Mel hurried into the classroom.

'Hi,' Lauren said.

'Hello,' Mel replied. Lauren noticed

that her voice was much quieter than usual.

Before they could say anything else, the bell rang and Mr Noland came into the classroom. 'Quiet, please!' he said, clapping his hands.

As Mr Noland took the register, Lauren watched Mel. She was looking pale and unhappy.

'OK, everyone, maths books out, please,' Mr Noland said as he put the register away. 'I'd like you to work through exercise three on page twenty-two.'

They fetched their maths books and quiet fell as everyone began working. Lauren could see that Mel was staring at the page of fractions, a panicky look on her face.

'Are you stuck?' Lauren whispered to her. 'I can help if you like.'

'No . . . no, I'm just thinking,' Mel replied as she hastily scribbled down an answer.

Lauren wracked her brains. She wanted to help Mel, but how?

'You don't seem to have done very much, Lauren.' Mr Noland's voice behind her made Lauren jump. 'Do you need some help?'

Lauren looked up guiltily. 'No, I'm fine . . .' she started to say but then she stopped. She'd had an idea. 'Actually, I do need help, please,' she said quickly. 'I'm confused.'

Mr Noland looked surprised. 'But you've been managing fractions OK all week. What seems to be the problem?' He leaned over her desk. 'All you have to do is put the fractions in order, smallest first. You need to consider both the denominator and the numerator –'

'The numerator is the number on top of the fraction and the denominator is the number on the bottom of the fraction, isn't it?' Lauren said, stopping him before he could race on ahead like he usually did.

'Yes and –'

'A fraction is just a small part of a whole, isn't it, Mr Noland?' Lauren said quickly. 'Like one piece of a whole cake. The denominator – the bottom number – tells you how many pieces the cake has been cut into and the numerator – the top number – tells you how many pieces of cake you have.' She glanced quickly to the side and was relieved to see that Mel was listening.

'Yes, that's right,' said Mr Noland, starting to sound a bit impatient.

'So, if the fraction is one third – one over three – the denominator is three which means the cake has been cut into three pieces,' she went on.

'Yes,' Mr Noland replied. 'And if you see the fraction one fifth – one over five – the denominator is . . .?'

Before Lauren could answer, Mel spoke up. 'Five?'

Lauren and Mr Noland looked round.

'That's right, Mel,' Mr Noland said.

'Which means the cake has been cut into five pieces. And the fraction one tenth would mean the cake had been cut

into ten pieces,' Mel said, her eyes starting
to light up. 'One fifth is bigger than one
tenth because if you cut a cake into five
pieces, each slice of the cake is bigger
than if you'd cut it into ten pieces.'

'That's right,' Mr Noland said to her.

Mel's eyes were shining. 'It suddenly all makes sense.'

'Well, that's great,' Mr Noland said. 'How about you, Lauren? Do you understand now?'

'Me?' Lauren caught herself. 'Oh, yes. Thank you, Mr Noland.'

Mr Noland smiled. 'Well, I'm glad you're happier.'

Lauren looked at the relief on Mel's face and smiled. 'Yes,' she said, feeling warm inside. 'I'm much happier now!'

Lauren was still glowing when she got home after school. 'You should have seen Mel's face when she finally worked out fractions,' she told Twilight as she groomed him before tacking him up to take him out on a ride with Mel and her pony, Shadow. 'She looked so relieved.'

Twilight snorted. When he was a pony he couldn't talk to her, but Lauren knew he understood every word she said.

'It kind of made me think,' Lauren said as she cleaned out the curry-comb. 'I know we try and help people when they've got big problems – like helping Jessica when she was really upset about her dad getting remarried, but couldn't we also use your powers to help those with smaller problems too? Sometimes people get almost as upset over something little as over something big.'

She looked at Twilight. He looked as though he was listening hard. 'What do you think?'

Twilight nodded his head.

Lauren hugged him. 'It'll be evening soon,' she whispered. 'We can talk properly then.'

CHAPTER

Three

Lauren was untacking Twilight after her ride with Mel when Buddy and Max came charging down the path that led from the house to the paddock.

'We've been at obedience class,' Max burst out. 'Buddy was brilliant! The teacher said he was the best puppy there!'

'That's great,' Lauren said, smiling.

'He learned to sit and lie down and

stay,' said Max. 'Watch!' Taking a handful
of dog treats out of his pocket, Max
called Buddy. 'Buddy! Here, boy!'

Buddy trotted over. 'Sit!' Max said
firmly, holding the treat above Buddy's
head.

To Lauren's amazement, Buddy sat.

'And lie down,' Max said, lowering the
treat.

Buddy did as he was told. 'Now stay,'
Max said. He walked once round Buddy
and then gave him the treat. 'Good boy!'
he cried. 'You did it!'

'Wow,' Lauren said, impressed.

'I can't wait until tomorrow's class,'
Max said happily. 'We're going to learn
how to get the puppies to walk on a

lead. Here, boy,' he called to Buddy, who was snuffling happily in Twilight's grooming kit. 'Let's practise.'

'Maybe it would be best to give Buddy a rest,' Lauren suggested. 'Before he gets tired of learning. We could play hide and seek.'

It was a game that she and Max had just taught Buddy. One of them held the puppy while the other went and hid and then Buddy found them.

'OK,' Max said.

Lauren turned Twilight out in the paddock and then she and Max took it in turns to hide. Buddy found them every time. It was great fun and even Twilight stopped grazing to look.

'Twilight's watching us!' Max
exclaimed, as he tried to push Buddy off
his tummy. 'Buddy! Get off!' he cried as
Buddy licked his nose.

Twilight whinnied. Lauren smiled. It
sounded almost as though he were
laughing.

★

'I'm just going out to see Twilight, Mum,' Lauren said, pulling her trainers on after supper.

'OK, honey,' Mrs Foster replied. She stood up and looked over to where Max was playing with Buddy. 'Come on, Max, time for your bath.'

Lauren ran down to the paddock. She couldn't wait to find out what Twilight thought of her plan about helping people with little problems as well as big.

'So, what do you think?' she asked as soon as he was a unicorn again.

'It's a good idea,' Twilight answered. 'The more people we can help, the better.'

Lauren grinned in delight. 'I was hoping you'd say that!'

'There are some rocks of rose quartz over there,' Twilight said, nodding in the direction of a cluster of trees at the end of his paddock. 'We could check who needs help right now.'

'OK!' Lauren mounted and they cantered down the paddock. Not for the first time, Lauren felt thankful that Twilight's paddock was well hidden from the house. She and Twilight should be safe in the shadow of the trees.

'There they are,' Twilight said, pointing his horn at several small boulders under an oak tree.

'Let's see Mel first,' Lauren said eagerly.

Within a few seconds, a picture had appeared in the rock, showing Mel snuggled up to her mum on the sofa.

'She looks much happier,' Twilight said, pleased.

Lauren nodded. 'OK, let's try Jessica.'

Twilight said Jessica's name and the picture changed. Jessica was sitting in the kitchen talking to her dad. She was frowning. Lauren leaned forward to find out why Jessica was looking so miserable.

'But I really wanted a pony, Dad,' Jessica was saying.

'It'll be easier to find one in the summer holidays,' Mr Parker replied. 'We'll have more time.'

Lauren sighed. She knew Jessica

wanted a pony right now, but she didn't
see how she and Twilight could help with
that. She was about to ask him to look at
someone else when Jessica said something
that caught her attention.

'But I get left out, Dad,' she said.
'Lauren and Mel meet after school to go
riding together and I can't join in. Like
this afternoon, they went riding together
and I couldn't go with them.'

Lauren sat back. 'Did you hear that?'

Twilight nodded. 'It can't be much fun
for Jessica seeing you and Mel riding
together.' He shook his mane. 'But it's
easy to solve. When you and Mel next
meet up, ask Jessica to join you. You can
take it in turns to ride me and Shadow.'

'Good idea,' Lauren said. Fired up by thinking how easy it would be to solve Jessica's unhappiness, she looked at the rock again. 'OK, let's see if anyone else in my class is unhappy.' She started suggesting different names. A little niggling feeling ran through her. She knew she shouldn't really be listening in on other people's conversations. Still, it was for the best, wasn't it? It was so she could help them.

Lauren got so engrossed in seeing the other kids from her class going about their everyday lives — watching TV, reading, doing homework — that she almost forgot that she was supposed to be looking for someone who was unhappy.

She was relieved – everyone seemed to be doing just fine. She glanced at her watch. 'I hadn't realized it was so late.' She stood up. 'We've only got ten minutes before I have to go in. We'll just have time to have a very quick fly-round tonight.'

'Let's go then,' Twilight said, touching his horn to the rock and making the picture disappear. Lauren mounted and held on to his mane.

Twilight started to trot forward, but then suddenly stopped. 'I feel tired,' he said, sounding surprised.

'Tired?' Lauren echoed.

'Yes, sort of achy but . . . but . . .' Twilight looked confused. 'It's strange – I never normally feel tired when I'm a unicorn.'

'We don't have to fly tonight,' Lauren said, concerned. 'Maybe you're not well.'

'No, I'll be fine,' Twilight replied bravely. 'Let's try again.' He trotted forward and this time took off into the sky. Lauren felt the cool wind streaming against her face. She leaned forward. They were flying again!

But soon she started to feel worried. Twilight seemed to be going slower than usual. Normally he galloped and swooped lightly and easily, but tonight his movements felt heavy and slow.

'Are you OK?' she asked.

'I . . . I feel a little strange,' Twilight replied.

'Let's go down,' Lauren said quickly.

Twilight didn't argue. Turning, he flew back to the paddock.

As he landed, Lauren slid off his back. He was breathing heavily. 'What's wrong?' she asked.

'I don't know,' he answered.

'Maybe you're coming down with
some sort of bug,' Lauren said anxiously.
'Shall I get Dad to call the vet?'

Twilight shook his head. 'I don't feel
ill. Just tired. I'll probably be better in the
morning.'

'I'll turn you back into a pony and
make you a warm bran mash,' Lauren
said. 'That might help.'

Twilight nodded and Lauren said the
Undoing Spell. Then, going to the feed
room, she put several scoops of bran, a
handful of oats and some salt into a

bucket and added hot water. Mixing it all up, she carried it back to Twilight. 'Here, boy, eat this.'

Twilight whickered gratefully and plunged his nose into the bucket.

As he ate, Lauren kissed his head. *Oh, Twilight,* she thought, biting her lip, *please be OK.*

CHAPTER

Four

Lauren didn't sleep well that night. As soon as she woke up, she looked out of her window. Twilight was standing by the gate. Pulling on her clothes, Lauren hurried outside.

'Are you feeling better now?' she asked.

To her relief, Twilight nodded.

Lauren rubbed his forehead. 'I've been so worried,' she told him softly.

'I don't think I could bear you to be ill.'

'Do you want to go for a ride this
evening?' Mel asked Lauren as they got
their books out that morning.

'Yes – if Twilight's OK,' Lauren replied.

'What's the matter with him?' Jessica
asked, looking concerned.

'He didn't seem very well last night,'
Lauren said. 'He was tired.'

'Maybe he's got a cold,' Mel suggested.
'Shadow sometimes gets them. They
make him a bit quiet, but they're not
serious. So, do you want to meet up?' she
asked. 'We could ride at mine instead of
going out, then, if Twilight seems tired,
you can always go home.'

'OK,' Lauren replied. She happened to glance at Jessica and caught a look of unhappiness fleeting across her face. 'Hey, Jess,' Lauren said quickly, 'why don't you meet us as well? We can take it in turns to ride.'

'Yeah,' Mel said, looking at Jessica. 'That's a great idea.'

'Really? Are you sure you don't mind?' Jessica said hesitantly.

'Of course not,' Lauren told her and Mel shook her head.

'OK then,' Jessica said, smiling. 'Thanks. I'll see if Dad will drop me off.'

To Lauren's relief, Twilight seemed to be back to his normal self when she got home from school that afternoon. He whinnied when he saw her coming.

'Do you feel well enough to go round to Mel's?' she asked him.

Twilight nodded. Feeling much happier, Lauren groomed him and saddled up.

Jessica was already at Mel's house when Lauren and Twilight arrived and the three girls had lots of fun timing themselves as they took it in turns to ride Shadow and Twilight around an obstacle course in Shadow's paddock.

'I've had a great time,' Jessica said happily as they let the ponies graze afterwards while they ate home-made cookies.

'We'll have to do this again,' Lauren said. 'It's more fun when there are three of us.'

'Yeah, definitely,' Mel said. 'Until you get your own pony, you can ride Shadow as much as you like, Jess.'

'And Twilight,' Lauren said.

Jessica's eyes shone happily. 'Thanks, guys. You're the best friends ever!'

'Jessica really enjoyed herself today,' Lauren said to Twilight that night after she had turned him into a unicorn.

'I'm glad we found out that she was upset,' Twilight said.

Lauren nodded. 'Let's have a look and see if there's anyone else who needs our help.'

They went down to the end of the field where the rose-quartz rocks were. The first person Lauren and Twilight saw was a boy in her class, David Andrews, with his father.

'They look like they're arguing,' Lauren

said, leaning closer to the rock.

'I'm not going to wear them!' David was saying.

'Yes, you are,' his dad replied firmly. 'And I've written to Mr Noland asking him to make sure that you do.'

'Dad!' David cried.

'It's for the best,' his dad said. He shook his head. 'David, lots of people wear glasses . . .'

Lauren looked at Twilight. 'Glasses!' she exclaimed. 'That's all that's upsetting David – he's got to wear glasses.'

'Well, if you tell him how good his glasses look, it might help,' Twilight suggested.

'It's worth a try,' Lauren agreed. 'Come

on, let's look at some other people.'

Most of the other kids seemed happy enough, apart from Joanne Bailey. Joanne sat at the table next to Lauren and she was miserable because her computer had broken down. She couldn't do the geography research that Mr Noland had asked them to do by the next day.

'I can easily help with that,' Lauren said. 'I'll print out some extra research from the Internet and take it in tomorrow for Joanne to use –'

'Lauren,' Twilight interrupted. 'I . . . I feel strange again.'

Lauren looked at him in concern. 'It's my fault. I shouldn't have made you do that obstacle course at Mel's.'

'But I was feeling all right then,' Twilight said. 'It's just now – I feel tired all of a sudden.' He shook his head wearily. 'Can we stop doing the magic now? I think I'd better change back.'

'Of course,' Lauren said, jumping to her feet.

Once Twilight was a pony again, he lay down. Lauren watched him, feeling very worried. What was the matter with him? He was never tired or ill. And this was twice now in two days.

'I'll leave my window open tonight,' she whispered. 'Whinny if you want anything and I'll come straight down.'

Twilight snorted softly and closed his eyes.

Lauren kept her window open all night just as she had promised. At six o'clock, she jumped out of bed and crossed the room to look out. But Twilight wasn't by the gate. Lauren felt alarmed. Twilight always stood there in the morning.

Pulling on her jeans, she hurried outside.

As she reached the paddock, she saw Twilight still lying where she had left him. His nose was resting heavily on the ground and his eyes were closed.

'Twilight!' Lauren cried out.

Twilight's ears flickered and he half-raised his head. He looked exhausted.

Lauren scrambled over the gate and raced across the grass. Throwing herself down on the ground beside him, she touched his neck. 'Twilight!' she gasped. 'What's the matter? You look really ill!'

Twilight snorted weakly.

'I'm going to get Dad!' Lauren said, jumping to her feet. 'Don't worry, Twilight. I'll be back as soon as I can.'

CHAPTER

Five

M r Foster was very worried when he saw Twilight. 'I'm going to call the vet,' he said.

As he hurried off, Lauren crouched down beside her pony. 'You're going to be OK,' she told him, her eyes stinging with hot tears. 'We'll find out what's wrong with you, I promise.'

Tony Blackstone, their vet, arrived

within the hour. He took Twilight's temperature and monitored his heart rate, then he ran his hands all over Twilight's body.

'Has Twilight been off-colour for a while?' he asked Lauren.

'He seemed tired the day before yesterday,' she replied, 'but otherwise he's been fine.'

'So he hasn't had a cough, or runny nose, or been restless and wanting to roll?'

'No,' Lauren replied.

Tony continued his examination, but at last he shook his head. 'Well, it's puzzling. If it weren't for the way he's acting, I'd say he seems to be a very healthy pony. I'll take a blood test and see what shows up.

Maybe he's got a virus.'

'Is there anything we can do?' Mr
Foster asked.

'Call me if he gets any worse, but
otherwise just let him rest. I'll ring you

with the test results as soon as I have them.' Tony shot Lauren a comforting glance. 'Don't worry. I'm sure he's going to be just fine.'

Lauren thought about Twilight all the way to school. What if there was something seriously wrong with him? A cold feeling clenched at her heart.

Walking into the cloakroom, she saw Joanne Bailey talking to her friend, Rachel. Lauren suddenly remembered about the extra research that she had printed out. 'Hi,' she said to them, as she put her coat on the peg. 'Did you do the geography homework last night?'

'Yeah,' Rachel replied.

'I couldn't,' Joanne said. 'My computer broke down.'

'I've got some extra if you need some more,' Lauren offered eagerly.

'It's OK, thanks,' Joanne replied. 'Rachel's lent me some of hers.'

'Are you sure?' Lauren asked, taking out the papers. 'I have them right here.'

'No, really, I'm fine,' Joanne said, and turned back to continue her conversation with Rachel.

Feeling disappointed that her plan to help hadn't worked out as she'd hoped, Lauren went into the classroom. As she walked through the door, she saw David talking with a group of his friends. She stopped. David had his new glasses on

but, to her relief, his friends didn't seem
to be teasing him.

Just then, David glanced up and caught
her watching him. 'What are you looking
at?' he asked suspiciously.

'Nothing,' Lauren replied.

'It must be your glasses,' one of David's
friends sniggered.

'It isn't!' Lauren said quickly, seeing
David go red. 'They're . . . they're very
nice glasses.'

David's friends burst out laughing.

'Lauren likes you, David!' one of them
said.

'Lauren Foster wants to be your
girlfriend.'

'No, I don't!' Lauren exclaimed.

She hurried to her desk, her own cheeks burning. As she went, she could hear David's friends start to tease him about how girls really liked boys with glasses. *Oh, great,* Lauren thought in dismay. *I haven't helped David at all — in*

fact, it looks like I've made things worse!

To her relief, Mel and Jessica arrived and she didn't have to listen to David's friends any more.

After school, Lauren went straight to see Twilight. To her relief, he whinnied when he saw her and trotted over to the gate. Lauren's heart rose. He looked much happier.

She got out her grooming kit and spent ages brushing him and combing out every tangle in his mane and tail. As she worked, she told him about David and Joanne. 'They didn't seem to need my help,' she said. 'In fact, I think I made things worse for David by saying that his glasses were nice. His friends started teasing him then.' She sighed. 'I wish you could talk back, but I won't turn you into a unicorn tonight. You've got to rest.'

Twilight nuzzled her.

'I'm going to go and get you some carrots,' Lauren said. 'I'll be back in a minute.'

She hurried to the house. Her dad was in the kitchen with Max. They had just got back from dog-training class and Max was putting Buddy's lead away.

Lauren took three carrots from the fridge. Buddy came over to see what she was doing. She patted him. 'How was Buddy's lesson? Is he still top of the class?'

'No,' Max said, stomping over and sitting down. 'No, he isn't.' Buddy tried to put his head on Max's knee, but Max pushed him away.

Mr Foster sighed. 'Buddy wasn't very good today,' he explained to Lauren. 'They were trying to teach the puppies to fetch a toy, but Buddy just kept running off and not coming back.'

Max stared at the floor.

'Don't worry,' Lauren said sympathetically. 'I'm sure Buddy will learn soon.'

'Lauren's right, Max,' Mr Foster said. 'You've got all weekend to teach Buddy how to fetch. There isn't another class until Monday.'

Lauren bent down and stroked the puppy. 'He'll learn to fetch, won't you, Buddy?'

Looking up at her, Buddy wagged his tail.

The next morning, Tony Blackstone came to check on Twilight again. 'Nothing obvious has shown up on the blood test,' he told Lauren and Mr Foster, 'but I'll send it off to the lab for further analysis. Still, I'm sure there's nothing to worry about. He looks better already, don't you, boy?'

Twilight whickered.

Tony smiled. 'You'd almost think he could understand what I was saying.'

Lauren only just managed to hide her grin. *If only he knew!* 'Should he rest today?' she asked.

'Yes, just to be on the safe side,' Tony said.

As Mr Foster walked with the vet back to his car, Max picked up a stick and threw it. 'Go, boy!' he called to Buddy. 'Go fetch!'

Buddy bounded up to the stick and grabbed it.

'That's it! Bring it here, Buddy!' Max called.

Buddy wagged his tail, the stick firmly clenched in his teeth.

'Buddy, come here!' Max said, his voice rising in exasperation. He started to walk

towards the puppy, but Buddy dodged
around Max and gambolled away up the
path.

'Buddy!' Max shouted crossly. 'Come
back!'

But Buddy ignored him and galloped
out of sight.

'You could try keeping him on a lead,'

Lauren suggested as Max stared after him.
'Then he couldn't get away.'

'I *know* how to train him, Lauren,' Max
snapped. 'You don't need to tell me.'

'I was only trying to help,' Lauren told
him.

'Well, I don't need your help!' Max
said. 'I —'

Mrs Foster appeared at the top of the path. 'Max!' she interrupted them. 'Can you go and get your swimming things, please? We don't want to be late.'

Max ran off as Mrs Foster walked down to Lauren. 'Do you want to come into town with us, honey?'

Lauren shook her head. 'I'll stay here with Twilight.'

'OK,' her mum said. 'Dad's around. If you need anything, just ask.'

After her mum and Max had driven away, Lauren groomed Twilight and then set to work cleaning his tack and tidying the tack room. By mid-morning everything was spotless.

Lauren went down to the paddock where Twilight was grazing. She sighed. There wasn't much else she could do. Unless . . .

Lauren looked round. Her dad was out on the farm and there was no one else nearby. If she turned Twilight into a unicorn, they could at least talk. Maybe they could even look to see if there were some more people to help. That wouldn't be too tiring. All he'd have to do was touch his horn to a rock.

She led Twilight to the shadow of the trees and said the magic words.

'So, how are you feeling?' she asked as soon as Twilight was a unicorn again.

'Not too bad,' Twilight answered. 'Just a

bit weak and . . .' He pawed at the ground with his hoof. 'Anyway, I'm feeling better than I did yesterday.'

'I was so frightened,' Lauren said. 'I thought you were terribly ill.' She looked towards the bottom of the field. 'Can we go and use your magic powers? I want to see if there's anyone else I can help.' She sighed. 'I didn't exactly do that well with David and Joanne yesterday.'

'At least you tried,' Twilight said reassuringly.

'I guess,' Lauren said as they went over to one of the rocks.

'When will your mum and Max be back?' Twilight asked.

'Probably not for ages yet,' Lauren

replied. 'But we could check and see where they are just to be on the safe side.'

Twilight nodded and, touching his horn to a rock, he murmured, 'Mrs Foster and Max.'

The picture in the rock showed Mrs Foster and Max having a drink in town. Lauren leaned closer. 'I'm never going to get Buddy to fetch,' Max was saying.

'Oh, Max!' Mrs Foster said. 'You've only been trying for one day. Just be patient.'

'Poor Max,' Lauren said to Twilight. 'He's really unhappy that Buddy won't –' She broke off. 'I've had an idea!' she said, her eyes widening. 'Why don't I teach

Buddy to fetch? Just think how pleased
Max would be to get back and find that
Buddy could do it after all!'

Twilight didn't answer. He was rubbing
his head against his leg as if it hurt.

Lauren looked at him in concern. 'Are
you OK?'

'I'm feeling strange,' Twilight replied
weakly. 'I think I need to rest.'

'I'll turn you back,' Lauren said
immediately.

As soon as Twilight was a pony again
he sighed and half-shut his eyes.

Lauren stroked his face. 'Do you want
anything?'

Twilight shook his head.

'OK,' Lauren said. 'Well, I'll be by the

stable with Buddy. If you need me, just whinny.'

She went to find Buddy. The puppy was asleep in the kitchen. He got up eagerly when Lauren came in.

'Come on, boy,' Lauren said, taking a packet of dog treats, a long dog lead and a toy from the cupboard. 'I'm going to teach you to fetch.'

Taking Buddy outside, she clipped on his lead. 'I'm going to throw this toy,' she told him. 'And I want you to bring it back.'

Buddy woofed in excitement as he looked at the orange plastic duck in her hand.

'Go on then, boy,' Lauren said,

throwing the
toy. 'Go fetch!'

Buddy raced after the
duck, grabbed it and then, just as he had
done with Max, he started to bound
away. But this time, the lead pulled him
up short. He stopped in surprise and
shook his head.

Lauren held out a dog treat. 'Here, boy,'
she encouraged.

Buddy looked at her and tried to back off but the lead held him tight.

Lauren waved the dog treat. 'Come on, Buddy.'

Buddy hesitated for a moment and then seemed to make up his mind. Still holding the toy, he trotted over to her.

'Good boy!' Lauren cried as he dropped the plastic duck and eagerly gobbled up the treat. She made a fuss of him and then stood up. 'OK. Let's try that again.'

Twenty minutes later, Buddy had got the hang of fetching the toy. As soon as he picked it up, he carried it back to Lauren, knowing that a treat was waiting for him.

'You are *such* a clever boy,' Lauren praised him after he had done it without the lead attached. 'Max is going to be so pleased!'

Buddy wagged his tail and, leaving him to play, Lauren went back to check on Twilight.

He was lying down in the paddock. Lauren knelt down beside him. 'Twilight? How are you feeling? Shall I get Dad to call the vet?'

Twilight shook his head and rested his muzzle on her knees.

'Oh, Twilight,' Lauren said. 'I wish I knew what the matter was.' She massaged his ears and he sighed.

⋆

Lauren wasn't sure how long she'd been sitting with Twilight when the silence was broken by the sound of Max's voice.

'Buddy! Where are you?' Max came running down the path to the paddock. Buddy woofed in delight and bounded over to say hello.

Seeing Twilight lying down, Max stopped in concern. 'Is Twilight sick again, Lauren?'

Lauren stood up. Her legs felt stiff from sitting on the ground for so long. 'He just seems tired.'

'Poor Twilight,' Max said. 'I hope he gets better soon.' He patted Buddy. 'Come on, Buddy. Now that I'm back I'm going to teach you to fetch.'

Lauren remembered her good news.
'You don't have to,' she said, smiling.

'What do you mean?' Max said in
surprise.

'I taught him while you were out.
Watch this.' Seeing the toy duck lying by
the gate, Lauren picked it up and threw
it. 'Fetch, Buddy!'

Buddy trotted over, picked the duck
up and brought it back. 'Good boy!'
Lauren exclaimed, feeding him a dog
treat from her pocket.

She turned to Max, her eyes shining.
'What do you think?'

To her surprise, she saw Max was
frowning crossly at her. 'But Buddy's my
dog. I wanted to teach him!' he cried.

'I was just trying to help,'
Lauren said.

'No, you weren't.' Max
looked close to tears. 'You just
wanted to show that you
could do it and I
couldn't!'

'Max —' Lauren began.

But Max wouldn't listen. 'You always interfere, Lauren! You always ruin things!' Pushing past her, he ran off into the woods at the side of the paddock.

Lauren watched him go, feeling awful. She wanted Max to be pleased. She hadn't meant to upset him. But now that she thought about it, she could see what he meant. Perhaps training Buddy hadn't been a good idea. How would she feel if someone had done the same thing with Twilight? She wondered whether to go after him, but decided it was best to leave him until he'd calmed down.

With a sigh, she turned and went to find her mum to tell her about Twilight.

✶

'I'll call Tony,' Mrs Foster said, looking at Twilight lying down in his field. 'Have you been riding this morning?'

'No, we just –' Lauren broke off. 'Well, we just stayed in the field.'

'So there's no reason why he should be tired,' Mrs Foster said.

Lauren shook her head. All Twilight had done that morning was some magic. A thought struck her and she almost gasped out loud. *Magic!* Of course! Why hadn't she thought about it before?

CHAPTER

Six

Lauren's thoughts raced. Every time
Twilight had started feeling strange,
he had been in his unicorn form doing
magic. Maybe he had some sort of special
unicorn illness. That would explain why
Tony Blackstone couldn't find anything
wrong with him!

As her mum went back to the house
to ring the vet, Lauren ran to Twilight.

'Twilight!' she said urgently.

Twilight looked up.

'I've had an idea. Maybe it's not the pony bit of you that's sick,' she said, 'maybe it's the *unicorn* bit! You always seem to be ill just after we've done some magic.'

Twilight looked thoughtful but Lauren couldn't tell exactly what he was thinking. She was filled with frustration. If only she could turn him into a unicorn and ask him what he thought, but she couldn't. Not in the middle of his field in broad daylight with her mum around. Then she had an idea.

'Maybe my book on unicorns will have something on unicorn illnesses,' she said. 'After all, that's where I found the words for the Turning Spell.'

Twilight bowed his head, as if in agreement.

'I'll be back later,' she said, almost running into her mum coming in the opposite direction.

'What's the matter?' her mum said in alarm. 'Has Twilight got worse?'

'No,' Lauren said. 'There's no change in him.'

'Well, I spoke to Tony,' her mum said. 'He's out on call at the moment and can't come over, but he said he'll ring in a few hours and see if there's any improvement.'

Lauren nodded. 'Thanks, Mum.' And before her mum could ask her what she was doing she raced on to the house and up to her bedroom. There she picked up the battered blue book lying by her bed and sat down. Turning to the front page, she scanned down the five chapter headings.

Chapter One:
Noah and the Unicorns
Chapter Two:
Arcadia
Chapter Three:
Unicorn Myths
Chapter Four:
Unicorn Habits
Chapter Five:
Unicorns and Humans

Lauren frowned. None of them seemed
to be about illnesses. She looked at the
list again. She knew the first chapter
about Noah and the unicorns almost by
heart now, but maybe one of the others
might have something useful in them.
Opening the book at the second chapter,
she started to read.

Half an hour later, a knock at the door
made her look up. 'Lauren?' her mum
said, looking round the door. 'Have you
seen Max?'

'No.' Lauren's head was swirling with
unicorn facts. 'No, I haven't.'

'He must be outside somewhere with
Buddy,' Mrs Foster said. 'I'll call him. It'll

be lunchtime in five minutes.'

Lauren nodded. She just had a few more pages to read.

Mrs Foster left and Lauren turned back to the last chapter. She hadn't found out anything about unicorn illnesses and she was starting to feel increasingly desperate. The last chapter was all about what unicorns did on Earth. Lauren skimmed over the words. She knew most of it already. She read the last paragraph.

Magic is a very powerful force. It must be used wisely or it will exact a powerful toll. Only when a unicorn's powers are used to help those who are truly in need, will the unicorn be strengthened and his powers replenished.

Lauren frowned at the words. What did
they mean? She thought she understood
the last sentence – if Twilight did good,
then he would become stronger. Well,
that was all right. They'd been doing
loads of good recently. He should be
extra strong.

'Lauren!' her mum called from
downstairs. 'Can you come here, please?'

Lauren sighed and shut the book. She'd
found out absolutely nothing about
unicorns getting ill. Maybe they *didn't* get
sick. Maybe her idea had been wrong
after all.

She walked slowly downstairs. As she
went into the kitchen, she stopped in
surprise. She'd been expecting to see Max

and her mum sitting at the table ready to eat lunch. But there was no sign of Max, and her mum was standing by the sink, looking worried.

'I can't find Max anywhere,' Mrs Foster said. 'I've been calling him, but he hasn't come in.'

Lauren frowned. 'Maybe he's playing with Buddy.'

'Buddy's here,' her mum said, pointing under the table.

Lauren's stomach tightened. Max hardly ever went off without his puppy.

'When did you last see him?' Mrs Foster asked her.

'It was just after you got back from swimming,' Lauren replied. Just then, she remembered the argument and her cheeks flushed. 'We had a bit of a fight.'

'What sort of a fight?' her mum asked quickly.

'I'd taught Buddy to fetch while you were out,' Lauren said. 'I was just trying to help but Max got really cross and ran off into the woods. I didn't mean to upset him, Mum.'

'Oh, Lauren,' Mrs Foster sighed. 'I understand, but I can see why Max got angry. It's hard for him being the youngest. Sometimes it must seem to him as if you do everything before him. Training Buddy is the first thing he's ever done on his own.'

'I know, I should have realized,' Lauren said regretfully.

'I'd better call your dad on his mobile phone,' Mrs Foster said. 'Perhaps Max is with him.'

Lauren watched anxiously as her mum made the call. She could tell from her face that it wasn't good news.

Mrs Foster replaced the receiver. 'Your dad hasn't seen Max. He's coming back to help us look.' She twisted her hands together. 'Which way did Max go when he ran off, Lauren?'

'Into the woods,' Lauren replied.

'That must have been about an hour and a half ago,' Mrs Foster said, checking her watch. 'I'll try ringing his friends. Maybe he went to one of their houses. Otherwise we'd better start searching.'

None of Max's friends had seen him, and when Mr Foster got back he and two of the farmhands, Tom and Hank, set out to look in the woods.

'Max could be anywhere,' Mrs Foster

said to Lauren. 'He could still be walking or he might be hiding or . . .' her voice faltered, 'he might be hurt.'

'It'll be OK, Mum,' Lauren said quickly. An idea had come to her.

Mrs Foster nodded and took a deep breath. 'Yes, you're right,' she said, as if she were trying to convince herself. 'It will.' She shook her head. 'Oh, if only we knew which direction he'd gone. I just want him home.'

'I . . . I'm just going to see Twilight,' Lauren said.

Mrs Foster nodded distractedly. 'I'll stay by the phone.'

Lauren ran down to Twilight's field. Twilight had stood up and was by the gate.

'Twilight!' Lauren burst out. 'I know you're not well, but Max has run away and no one knows where he is — I really need your help. Please can I turn you into a unicorn? It would just be for a few minutes so that you can use your magic to see if we can find out where Max is. I wouldn't ask but . . .'

Twilight was already nodding his head up and down.

'Oh, thank you!' Lauren gasped.

Twilight started to trot to the trees. Lauren ran after him. As soon as they reached the safety of the shadows, Lauren said the magic words.

As she spoke the last line of the verse, she tensed expectantly.

There was a pause. For one awful
moment, Lauren thought that the spell
wasn't going to work, but then there was
a weak purple flash and Twilight was
suddenly a unicorn again.

'What happened then?' Lauren gasped.

'I don't know. It felt very strange,' Twilight replied, looking confused.

'I thought you weren't going to change,' Lauren said, her heart pounding.

'Let's not worry about it now,' Twilight said quickly. 'We need to find out where Max is.' He touched his horn to the nearest rose-quartz rock. 'I want to see Max!'

Lauren and Twilight waited. They looked at each other.

Nothing had happened!

CHAPTER

Seven

'It hasn't worked,' Lauren said, looking round. 'Maybe it's the wrong sort of rock. Try that one.' She pointed desperately to another.

Twilight trotted over. 'Max!' he said, touching his horn to the hard surface.

Again, nothing. Lauren looked horrified.

'Your magic's not working!' she exclaimed.

Twilight looked totally bewildered. 'I don't feel right. I feel drained, as if,' he looked at her in alarm, 'as if all my magic's been used up.'

His words sent a shock through Lauren. 'Used up? But it can't be!'

'That's how it feels,' Twilight said.

'But the unicorn book said that when unicorns do good they get stronger and their magic gets replenished,' Lauren said. 'We've been doing lots of good deeds. You should have loads of magic.'

'What did it say *exactly*?' Twilight asked urgently.

Lauren tried to remember. 'It was

something about how a unicorn's magic mustn't be used lightly. I'll go and get it!'

She raced back to the house and returned a few minutes later with the book. 'Here,' she said, and she read out the last paragraph.

Magic is a very powerful force. It must be used wisely or it will exact a powerful toll. Only when a unicorn's powers are used to help those who are truly in need, will the unicorn be strengthened and –

She broke off with a gasp. 'Oh no! That's it!'

'What?' Twilight demanded.

'Don't you see?' Lauren said, pointing to the book. 'We've been trying to help everyone with all their little everyday problems, not people who are truly in need, so your magic hasn't been strengthened, it's just been used up. A toll is something you pay; well, maybe you're having to pay for how we've been using your magic. Maybe that's why you've been feeling ill!'

Twilight stared at her. 'You might be right.'

Tears sprang to Lauren's eyes. 'What are we going to do? Now we really need your magic to help find Max, we can't use it because there's none left.'

Twilight nuzzled her. 'Don't worry. We can still help to find Max even if we can't use my magic. There must be another way.'

He pawed at the ground, as if trying to
think. A stick cracked beneath his hoof. 'I
know what to do!' he said suddenly. 'Get
Buddy and see if he can find Max.
Pretend it's hide and seek. Buddy is
brilliant at that!'

'Of course!' Lauren exclaimed.

'Turn me back into a pony and we can follow him to Max together,' Twilight said.

Lauren looked at Twilight in concern. 'But you're not well. You're too weak.'

'I don't care,' Twilight said, looking determined. 'I want to help you find your brother.'

'Are you sure?' Lauren said.

'Yes,' Twilight insisted. He nudged her with his nose. 'Come on, we're wasting time!'

Lauren didn't argue with him any longer. She turned him back into a pony, then she went into the house to tell her mother her plan, before fetching Buddy.

'We're going to find Max,' she told the

puppy. She saddled Twilight and led him and Buddy to the place where she had last seen Max.

'Find Max, boy,' she said to Buddy. 'Good dog. Off you go.'

Buddy put his nose to the ground and began to snuffle round. Suddenly he seemed to pick up Max's scent. With a woof, he bounded up the path and into the woods. Lauren mounted Twilight and they trotted after him.

Lauren's heart was beating fast as they entered the trees. What if this idea didn't work? What if they all got lost trying to find Max? She pushed the thoughts out of her mind and concentrated on encouraging Buddy.

'That's it!' she called to the puppy.
'Good boy!'

Buddy set off down a narrow trail
away from the main path. Lauren had to
duck under low-hanging branches as the
path twisted and turned. Brambles caught
at her jeans.

She frowned as she tried to work out
where they were. They seemed to be
heading in the direction of . . .

The gorge!

'Buddy! Be careful!' she gasped in
alarm. 'The path ends just ahead. It's
dangerous!'

But Buddy started to run even faster.
He disappeared from sight.

Lauren wondered what to do, but Twilight took the decision out of her hands. Breaking into a canter, he set off through the trees after the puppy. Lauren flung herself down against his neck. Clinging to Twilight's mane, she looked ahead as best she could.

Suddenly Lauren heard Buddy bark and then Twilight jerked to a stop. Her breath came in short gasps as she pushed herself upright in the saddle. Buddy was just ahead of them. He was standing beside a faded wooden sign that read:

**DANGER
KEEP BACK**

Her heart pounding, Lauren dismounted.

Twilight nuzzled her arm and she could tell he was also worried. Slipping the reins over her arms, she walked cautiously forward. She didn't dare walk right to the edge of the gorge in case the crumbling ground gave way. Letting go of Twilight, she dropped to her hands and knees and crawled the last few metres. She felt sick. What was she going to see when she looked over?

'Buddy!' she called as Buddy inched right to the edge. 'Be careful!'

'Lauren!' a faint voice called.

Lauren felt her heart leap. 'Max!' she gasped.

CHAPTER

Eight

T hrowing herself on to her stomach, she looked over the edge of the gorge. Max was crouched on a rocky ledge about four metres below the cliff edge. Beneath him, the gorge tumbled away steeply, ending in a pit of rocks and brambles far, far below. His eyes were wide with fear.

'Lauren,' he cried. 'You found me! I

didn't think anyone ever would.'

'Are you OK?' Lauren asked.

'Yes. I was having a look over the side of the gorge and the ground just sort of crumbled,' Max said. 'But I landed on this ledge. I'm OK. I just can't get back up.'

Lauren went cold as she thought about what might have happened if he hadn't landed on the outcrop.

'I'll go and get help!' she said.

'No! Don't leave me!' Max looked terrified.

Lauren looked desperately at her brother. 'I've got to go. I can't reach you.'

'I don't want to stay here alone,' Max said tearfully.

'But you wouldn't be alone,' Lauren

said desperately. 'Buddy's here.'

'Buddy!' Max gasped in delight. Buddy barked, as if in reply.

'Look, I'm going to have to go and get Mum and Dad, Max,' Lauren said. 'Buddy will stay with you.'

Max looked up. 'OK,' he said bravely.

'I'll be back as soon as I can,' Lauren promised.

Edging away from the cliff, she stood up, commanded Buddy to stay and ran to Twilight. 'Quick, Twilight!' she gasped as she mounted. 'We've got to get home!'

'Lauren! Where have you been? I've been out of mind with worry!' Mrs Foster came running down the path as Lauren and Twilight galloped out of the woods towards the farm. 'How could you have – ?'

'Mum! I've found Max,' Lauren interrupted her mother as Twilight slowed to a trot. 'He's stuck in the gorge.'

'Oh my goodness,' Mrs Foster said, going pale. 'The gorge!'

'He's all right,' Lauren said. 'He's on a ledge. Buddy's with him.'

'I'll ring your dad,' Mrs Foster said. 'He's in the woods.' She turned and ran back to the house.

'I'll go back there,' Lauren called after her. 'I told Max I'd get back as quickly as I could.'

Mrs Foster stopped. 'OK,' she agreed. 'If you get there before your dad, then tell Max that help will be along very soon.' She ran into the house.

'Are you OK to go back, boy?' Lauren asked Twilight.

He nodded and swung round, pulling eagerly at his bit. He suddenly seemed much livelier, almost as if he had got all his energy back. Lauren leaned forward and they cantered back into the woods again.

Lauren reached the gorge just as her dad, Tom and Hank jumped out of the pick-up truck.

'It's OK, Max,' she said, crawling to the edge. 'Dad's coming.'

'Thanks for getting help, Lauren,' murmured her brother.

'Lauren! Thank heavens you found
him!' Mr Foster said, hurrying to the
edge of the gorge. Lying down on his
stomach, he looked over. 'It's all right,
Max,' he said. 'We'll get you up.'

Lauren watched as Tom and Hank tied one end of a long coil of rope securely around a thick oak tree and then, using it to hold on to, her dad lowered himself over the edge.

'We're ready to come back up,' he called, once he had been down there for a few minutes.

There was a bit of shouting and then Tom and Hank began to pull on the rope. Mr Foster and Max soon scrambled over the edge of the gorge.

Lauren sighed with relief as her dad hugged Max as if he were never going to let him go. 'Oh, Max! Why did you go off like that?' he said.

'I'm sorry.' Max looked close to tears

again. 'I was just cross with Lauren. I'm really sorry, Dad.'

Mr Foster hugged him. 'Just don't do anything like it ever again.'

'I won't,' Max said, as Mr Foster put him down. Max looked at Lauren. 'I'm sorry I got upset with you, Lauren.'

'It's OK. I should have let you teach Buddy to fetch,' Lauren told him.

'I was being silly,' Max said. He looked at the ground. 'I'd . . . I'd like you to help me train Buddy if you want.'

Lauren smiled. 'You don't need me. You're doing fine on your own, Max. Anyway, I don't think Buddy needs much training,' she said, looking at the puppy. 'No dog could be cleverer. He was the one who found you.'

Max crouched down and hugged Buddy. 'Thanks, boy.' Buddy wagged his tail in delight.

'Come on, Max. Let's get you home,' Mr Foster said. 'The pick-up is just through the trees.' He looked at Lauren. 'Will you be OK riding back on your own?'

'I'll be fine,' she said. She waved as her dad, Hank, Tom and Max set off through the shadows. The pick-up started and Lauren listened as it drove away. Once the woods were quiet again, she took off Twilight's bridle and saddle. Then, taking a deep breath, she said the words of the Turning Spell.

Almost before the last word was out of her mouth, there was a bright purple flash and Twilight was a unicorn once more.

'Oh, Twilight,' she said, hugging him. 'Thank you for helping me.'

Twilight pushed his nose against her chest. 'I'm just glad Max is OK,' he said. 'I wish I could have used my magic to help you find him more quickly.'

'It doesn't matter now,' Lauren said. 'Your idea to use Buddy was brilliant. If you hadn't thought of that, Max might still be stuck. And anyway,' she went on quickly, 'it wasn't your fault that we couldn't use magic. It was mine. I was the one who used it all up by getting you to look at my friends.'

'You were only trying to help people,'
Twilight reminded her.

'I know,' Lauren said. 'But I didn't
really need magic for that. I could have
seen that Mel was upset about her
fractions and I should have realized that
Jessica was feeling left out, and the other
people I tried to help – Joanne, David,
Max – well, they didn't really need my
help at all.' She looked down. 'I think I
just liked feeling important.'

Twilight nuzzled her. 'Don't feel bad. It
turned out all right in the end.'

'Yes,' Lauren said slowly, 'thanks to you.
You're the best, Twilight. Even though
you were feeling really ill, you still let me
ride you so that we could follow Buddy

here.' She hugged him. 'How are you feeling now?'

Twilight considered the question. 'All right, actually. I don't feel tired at all.'

'Maybe it's because we've just helped Max,' Lauren suggested. 'Perhaps your powers have come back now that we've actually helped someone truly in need like the book said.'

'I'm sure that's what has happened,' Twilight said, tossing his head, 'because I feel great!' He pranced on the spot. 'Let's go flying, Lauren!'

'But it's not dark enough,' Lauren protested.

'I'll stay in the treetops,' Twilight said. He pushed her with his nose. 'Come on!

I want to fly!'

Lauren couldn't resist. 'OK then!' she said, scrambling on to his back.

'I could always use my magic . . .' Twilight began teasingly.

'Not a chance!' Lauren interrupted him with a grin. 'From now on we only use your magic powers to help people who truly need help. Agreed?'

'Agreed,' Twilight said. He started to trot out of the trees and then he stopped. 'Am I really the best?' he asked, almost shyly.

Lauren nodded as she hugged him. 'The very best,' she smiled.

My Secret Unicorn

A Special Friend

The pony looked at her
with sad dark eyes and a memory
stirred in Lauren's mind. The very first
time she had seen Twilight he had looked
at her in exactly the same way. It was so
weird ... A thought struck Lauren and
she almost gasped out loud. No, she
couldn't be right ...

To Michelle Misra – for making
My Secret Unicorn *so magical*

CHAPTER
One

'Lauren! Are you ready? The Parkers are here!' Mrs Foster said, looking out of the kitchen window.

Lauren fed the remains of her toast to Buddy, her brother Max's young Bernese mountain dog. He gobbled up the crusts with a gulp and then bounded round in front of her.

'Out of the way, Buddy!' Lauren said,

laughing. She grabbed her riding hat
from the table. 'See you later, Mum.'
'Have fun!' Mrs Foster called.

'I will.' Lauren hurried out of the
house to the car. Her friend Jessica sat in
the back with her stepsister, Samantha.
They were going to be choosing a pony
and Lauren was helping them!

'Hello, Lauren,' Mr Parker said,
smiling at her as she got into the back of
the car.

'Hi,' Lauren said. She exchanged grins
with Jessica and Samantha. They were
both looking very excited.

Mr Parker started the engine. 'OK,
everyone. High Meadows farm, here we
come.'

The stables were a fifteen-minute drive
from Lauren's house on the outskirts of

town. A signpost at the top of the farm's
drive read:

**High Meadows
– riding school and pony sales
Proprietor: T. Bradshaw**

At the end of the drive were two red
barns, an office and a large training ring.

As Mr Parker stopped the car, a
woman with curly auburn hair came out
of the office. 'Hi there,' she said, smiling
as they piled out of the car. 'You must be
the Parkers?'

Mr Parker nodded. 'Yes, this is
Samantha and Jessica and Jessica's friend,
Lauren.'

'I'm Tina Bradshaw,' the woman said. She glanced at Jessica and Samantha. 'So, you're looking for a pony?'

They both nodded.

Tina smiled. 'Then come with me – I have plenty for you to see.'

She led the way across the yard and into the first barn. On either side of the wide central aisle ponies peered over half doors, their ears pricked.

'I'll show you the ponies I think might be most suitable and then you can choose three or four you'd like to try out in the ring,' Tina said. She headed over to a stall where a chestnut with a white blaze was looking out. 'This is Puzzle. He's ten years old and a very good jumper.

Next to him is ...'

Lauren's brain was soon spinning with pony names. After looking at twelve ponies in the barn, Samantha and Jessica had chosen four to ride – Bullfinch, Puzzle, Lacey and Sandy. Tina saddled them and led them to the training ring.

'Why don't you try Puzzle first?' she said to Jessica, handing her the reins of

the chestnut. 'And Samantha, you try
Bullfinch.'

Lauren watched as Samantha and
Jessica took turns to ride the ponies
around the ring. All of them looked
lovely and she didn't know which one
she'd choose if it were up to her.

Seeing some ponies looking over the
gate of a field a little way off, Lauren
wandered over to see them. There was a
palomino – tan-coloured with a pale gold
mane and tail – a bay and a black. Lauren
stroked them and then she noticed
another pony – a shaggy little dapple-
grey – standing all by herself further up
the field.

Lauren stared. The dapple-grey was
exactly like her pony, Twilight! Although
Twilight looked like an ordinary pony, he
had an exciting secret. At certain times of
the day, Lauren could say the words of
the Turning Spell, which transformed
Twilight into a unicorn!

Lauren hurried round the fence. As she

got closer she saw that the dapple-grey pony was a bit smaller and scruffier than Twilight, but otherwise just like him. She even had the same pattern of dapples on her coat.

Lauren picked a handful of long grass. 'Here,' she called, holding the grass out. 'Here, girl.'

The grey mare lifted her head slightly.

'Come on,' Lauren encouraged.

The mare walked over. Stopping by the fence, she reached out and took the grass, her soft grey lips nuzzling Lauren's palm.

On her head-collar was a brass name-plate. 'Moonshine,' Lauren read out. 'Is that your name?'

The pony
looked at her
with sad dark
eyes and a
memory
stirred in
Lauren's mind. The very
first time she had seen Twilight
he had looked at her in exactly the same
way. It was so weird. He and this pony
were so alike they might almost be
brother and sister. A thought struck
Lauren and she almost gasped out loud.
No, she couldn't be right ...

'Moonshine, are ... are you a unicorn
in disguise, just like Twilight?' she
whispered.

CHAPTER
Two

Moonshine stared at Lauren.
'I know about unicorns,' Lauren
said quickly. 'I have one myself.'

'Lauren!' Hearing Jessica, Lauren
turned.

'Come and tell me which pony you
like best,' Jessica called to her.

Lauren didn't want to leave
Moonshine. 'Just a minute,' she replied.

She looked at the little grey pony again. 'I won't tell anyone,' she whispered. 'Please – are you a unicorn?'

Moonshine didn't move.

'Lauren!' Jessica called impatiently.

Lauren gave up on getting Moonshine to respond. 'Coming!' She hurried back to the ring, her thoughts racing.

Jessica was riding Sandy around the ring for a second time. Seeing Lauren coming over, she called out, 'Watch how Sandy goes and then you can tell me which pony you like best.'

Lauren nodded and went to stand by Tina at the gate.

Tina smiled at her. 'I saw you talking to Moonshine just now.'

'She's lovely,' Lauren said.

Tina nodded. 'I think so too, but no one ever wants to buy her. I guess she doesn't look flashy enough. It's a shame, she's got a heart of gold. You're not looking for a pony, are you?'

Lauren shook her head regretfully. She would have loved to buy Moonshine but she knew her parents would never agree.

'Pity,' Tina sighed. 'Moonshine could do with some love. The girls who help out here prefer riding the livelier ponies and she doesn't get much attention. Oh, well.' She turned away to speak to Mr Parker.

Jessica rode over. 'So, which do you like best?' she asked eagerly.

'I like them all,' Lauren said truthfully. She watched the palomino Jessica was riding. 'Sandy's very pretty.'

'She's my favourite,' Jessica confided. 'But I think Sam likes Bullfinch.' She looked curiously at Tina. 'What were you and Tina talking about?'

'About that pony over there,' Lauren

said, pointing to Moonshine who was still standing by the fence in the field.

Jessica stared. 'Isn't she sweet? She looks just like Twilight!'

Lauren nodded.

'I'll ask if we can try her out,' Jessica said.

Lauren felt a leap of excitement. If Moonshine was a unicorn and Jessica bought her, it would be brilliant! But to Lauren's disappointment, when Jessica asked, Tina shook her head.

'Moonshine will be too small for Samantha,' she told Jessica. 'She's only 12.2 hands high. You need a pony who's at least 13.2.'

'Oh,' Jessica said, looking at Lauren.

'OK, Samantha,' Mr Parker called.
'Come over here. It's decision time.'

Samantha rode over on Bullfinch.

'So which pony is it to be?' Mr Parker
asked her and Jessica.

'Sandy,' Jessica said immediately.

'Bullfinch,' said Samantha at the same
moment.

'Not Bullfinch,' Jessica put in quickly. 'He's too heavy and slow.'

'He's obedient and reliable,' Samantha said, patting the buckskin's neck. 'Not like Sandy. She refused when I tried to jump her.'

'She didn't with me,' Jessica said.

'Fluke,' Samantha said.

'It *wasn't*!' Jessica declared hotly.

'Sandy's only young,' Tina said. 'She's still learning about jumping, so she might stop a little more than an experienced pony. But once she gets used to jumps she should be just fine.'

'Well, I want Bullfinch,' Samantha announced.

'And I want Sandy!' Jessica frowned.

Mr Parker looked at Tina. 'I'm sorry about this – there seems to be some disagreement.'

'That's OK,' Tina said understandingly. 'Buying a pony is a big commitment. You have to be sure you're getting the right one. How about you talk it over tonight and come back tomorrow? You can try them both out again then.'

Mr Parker looked relieved. 'Are you sure that would be OK?'

Tina nodded. 'No problem.'

As soon as Lauren got home she raced to Twilight's field and told him all about Moonshine.

'So, what do you think?' she demanded

eagerly. 'Do you think she might be a unicorn?'

Twilight stamped a hoof. Lauren wished she could turn him into a unicorn so that they could speak properly, but she knew her dad was working nearby so she couldn't risk it.

'We'll talk about it tonight, when it starts
to get dark,' she promised.

It was nearly twilight and Lauren went
back to the house. She fetched a can of
lemonade from the fridge and went up to
her bedroom. This was her favourite
place in the whole house. It had a sloping
ceiling, and a large window with a
window seat which looked down on to
Twilight's paddock. Lauren looked out.
Twilight was grazing in the shade of the
trees. He looked happy. She blew him a
kiss before picking up an old blue book
that was lying on the window seat. It was
called *The Life of a Unicorn* and it had
been given to her by Mrs Fontana, an old
lady who owned a bookshop. Mrs

Fontana was the only person in the world who knew about Twilight.

Sitting down, Lauren curled her legs underneath her and carefully opened up the book. After Twilight, it was one of her most treasured possessions. In the back of it were the words of the Turning Spell.

Lauren leafed carefully through the book, her eyes scanning the yellowing, faded pages. At last, she found what she was looking for. A picture of a little grey pony. It was a unicorn in its pony form.

She turned back a page and read the words . . .

Descendants of the two young unicorns that Noah took on to the Ark still roam the Earth today. They look like small ponies. Each of them hopes to find someone who will learn how to free them from their mortal form.

Lauren turned again to the picture of the small grey pony. Both Twilight and Moonshine were just like it. Lauren stared out of the window, frowning slightly. Was Moonshine a unicorn? She and Twilight had to find out!

As soon as she could that evening, Lauren

rushed out to find Twilight. Quickly she
said the words of the Turning Spell that
changed him into a unicorn:

> *Twilight Star, Twilight Star,*
> *Twinkling high above so far.*
> *Shining light, shining bright,*
> *Will you grant my wish tonight?*
> *Let my little horse forlorn*
> *Be at last a unicorn!*

With a bright purple flash, Twilight stood
before her in his unicorn form.

'Well, what do you think?' Lauren
asked again.

'I need to see her before I can tell,'
Twilight replied.

'OK, let's fly over there now,' Lauren said. She looked up at the dusky sky. 'It's dark enough and Mum and Dad won't miss me. Mum's busy working and Dad's watching a film on TV.'

She scrambled on to Twilight's back and, with a snort, he jumped up into the sky. He cantered towards the sliver of moon that had started to shine above the trees.

'Which way is it?' Twilight asked.

'Just out of town, to the north,' Lauren said, her hair blowing back from her face. 'It should be really quick to fly there. The roads took us a very twisty way round.'

She was right. Flying direct, they

reached High Meadows farm in five minutes.

Lauren scanned the ground. The only things moving seemed to be ponies. Tina and her helpers had probably gone home for the night.

'I think we can go down,' she said to Twilight. 'It's that field over there by the training ring. Look, there she is – the little grey standing all by herself.'

As Twilight swooped down, the palomino, bay and black ponies scattered to the far side of the field with snorts of alarm. But Moonshine didn't move. She stared at Twilight as if transfixed. Her dark eyes grew wider and then she lifted her head and arched her neck. Shaking back

her mane, Moonshine stepped towards
Twilight, her delicate ears pricked, her
hooves moving daintily on the grass. She
looked so graceful with the moonlight
shining on her pale coat that Lauren
didn't need Twilight to tell her what he
thought. Moonshine *was* a unicorn. She
knew it beyond doubt.

Twilight whinnied softly. Moonshine
whickered back and as she reached him,
they extended their heads and touched
noses.

'Unicorn,' Lauren heard Twilight
murmur.

Moonshine snorted and looked at
Lauren.

'What's she saying?' Lauren asked.

'She's saying you told her that you had a unicorn,' Twilight translated. Moonshine whimpered sadly.

'She has never found anyone to be her Unicorn Friend,' Twilight said. 'It's all she's ever dreamed of.'

Lauren felt desperately sorry for the little pony. She knew that for a unicorn to be freed from its pony form, it needed to find a special person – a special person who believed in magic. Then they could share magical adventures together. 'Please tell her she will find someone to be her Unicorn Friend,' Lauren urged. She reached forward and patted Moonshine. 'You'll find someone who believes in magic. I know it.'

Lauren spoke determinedly but inside she was far from sure. *I hope I'm right,* she thought.

Moonshine bowed her head and snorted quietly.

'She says she doesn't think it will happen,' Twilight said softly.

Looking at the dejected little pony, Lauren wanted to help her more than anything else in the world. Sliding off Twilight's back, she went over and stroked Moonshine's neck to comfort her. Moonshine looked up at her, her dark eyes like deep forest pools.

Suddenly there was a change in her. Moonshine's ears pricked and she stiffened. She glanced round to the gate and then, turning back to Twilight, she snorted anxiously.

Lauren saw a look of alarm cross Twilight's face.

'Quick, Lauren,' he said. 'There's someone coming!'

CHAPTER

Three

'Over there!' Lauren said, pointing to a nearby copse.

Lauren swiftly mounted and Twilight galloped among the trees. They were only just in time. As they reached the shadows, they saw a boy walk up to the gate and climb over it. Lauren and Twilight waited in the trees, watching without being seen.

The boy headed towards Moonshine.

He was skinny with untidy dark hair. He
wasn't very tall but, judging by his face,
Lauren guessed that he was probably
about her age.

'Here, Moonshine,' she heard him say.
He held out a handful of carrots. 'Here,
beauty.'

Moonshine walked over to the boy. He fed her the carrots and stroked her tangled mane. 'Did you think I wasn't coming?'

Moonshine snorted.

Lauren bent low on Twilight's neck. 'Who is he?' she whispered. 'Did Moonshine say?'

'She doesn't know,' Twilight replied. 'She told me he started coming a few days ago – he's here for the summer with his family. He always brings her something to eat and just spends time talking to her and stroking her. Moonshine likes him.'

Lauren watched the boy talking softly to Moonshine and suddenly made a decision. 'Wait here,' she said to Twilight as she dismounted and walked out of the trees.

The boy almost jumped out of his skin. He stared at her in surprise and then turned and began to run down the field.

'Please, wait!' Lauren called, chasing after him.

But the boy didn't stop. He raced to the gate.

'Wait!' Lauren implored him, panting for breath as she ran after him. 'I only want to talk to you!'

Glancing over his shoulder, the boy tripped over a tree root and fell. It gave Lauren the time she needed to catch up with him. She grabbed his arm.

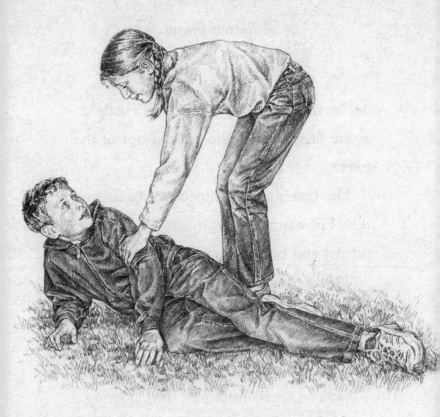

'I wasn't doing anything!' he gasped, his face pale, his brown shock of hair sticking up. 'I was just talking to the pony. I wasn't hurting her, I promise.'

'I know you weren't,' Lauren said. 'It's OK.'

The boy stared at her properly for the first time. 'You're ... you're not angry with me for feeding her?'

'No,' Lauren said in surprise. 'Of course not.' She let him go and they both stood up.

'Is it your pony?' he asked.

Lauren shook her head. 'No. She belongs to Tina, the woman who owns these stables.' She frowned. 'Who are you? What are you doing here?'

'My name's Michael,' the boy said warily. 'If Moonshine's not your pony, what are *you* doing in the field?'

Lauren didn't know what to reply. 'I ... er ... I was here today,' she said, 'with some friends who are buying a pony. I saw Moonshine and liked her.

I thought I'd come back and visit.' At
least it was half the truth.

Michael relaxed and, for the first time,
he smiled at her. 'That's why I'm here
too,' he confessed. 'I was exploring a few
days ago and I saw Moonshine in the
field. I thought she looked kind of lonely
so I started to visit her. I've been coming
every day. So, where do you live?'
Michael asked out of curiosity.

'Not too far away,' Lauren said vaguely,
thinking: *if you fly here.* 'How about you?'
she asked, changing the subject.

'Me?' Michael hesitated for a moment.
'In Washington,' he replied. 'Only I'm
staying in a house nearby for the summer
with my mum and dad. We've done a

house swap with a colleague of Jodie's …
I mean my mum's.' He glanced at her,
wondering whether to say more. 'Jodie's
my adopted mum,' Michael explained
after a pause. 'I haven't been with them
long. My real mum died two years ago
and I was put into foster care.'

Lauren didn't know what to say. 'I'm
really sorry,' she stammered.

Michael gazed down. 'It's OK.'

He looked up and smiled as
Moonshine walked over to him, her
hooves echoing softly on the grass.

Moonshine snorted softly and rubbed
her head against Michael's chest. He
scratched her ears. There was silence for a
moment.

'It must be strange moving to the country just for the summer,' Lauren said sympathetically.

'Yes, it is,' Michael admitted. 'It's hard to fit in and make new friends when everyone's already settled.' He tried to look cheerful. 'But at least I get to see horses – you don't see many of them in the city.' He stroked Moonshine's face. 'I really wish I could have a pony of my own. I stayed on a farm for a while when I was being fostered. The people there taught me to ride. I love horses.'

'Me too,' Lauren said. 'Moonshine's for sale, you know,' she added carefully. She knew she'd only just met Michael but she was already beginning to think that he might make a good Unicorn Friend.

'For sale?' Michael echoed. His face lit up briefly then faded. 'Jodie and Chris – Mum and Dad – would never buy her for me.'

'Well, ponies are expensive to buy and look after,' Lauren agreed.

Michael shook his head. 'Oh, it's not the money. It's just they're not horsey people. When I started living with them I asked if I could go to a riding school, but they didn't take me seriously. They said that I would get bored and offered to buy me a bike and a skateboard instead.'

Michael looked sadly at Moonshine. 'Jodie and Chris are really nice, but they don't understand me at all . . .' He broke off, as if he'd said too much. 'Look, I'd better go,' he muttered. 'I'll see you.'

'I'm Lauren,' Lauren said, realizing she hadn't told him her name.

'See you, Lauren,' Michael said and immediately set off at a run.

'Wait! Where do you live?' Lauren called after him.

But Michael didn't stop. Climbing over the gate, he disappeared into the darkness. Lauren stared after him until she heard a familiar whicker.

Looking round, she saw Twilight walking out from the cover of the trees. It was clear from his expression that he had heard everything.

'Michael doesn't sound very happy,' he said, joining Lauren and Moonshine.

Lauren shook her head. 'No. It must be difficult having to get used to new parents and not knowing anyone round here.'

'Apart from Moonshine,' Twilight said, nuzzling the grey pony, who nuzzled him back before staring wistfully after

Michael. She whickered softly.

'Moonshine says she really likes him,' Twilight said. 'He's kind and gentle.'

'And lonely,' Lauren said. She sighed and looked at the little grey pony. Both Moonshine and Michael were so unhappy. She wished she and Twilight could help. But what could they do?

Four

The following morning, Lauren had just finished her breakfast when Mr Parker arrived. As she got into the back of his car, it was obvious that Jessica and Samantha hadn't come to an agreement on which pony they should have. They were sitting, their arms crossed, arguing with each other.

'We're getting Bullfinch,' Samantha

was saying.

Jessica frowned. 'No, Sandy.'

'That's enough, you two,' Mr Parker warned. 'The idea of buying a pony was that you would have something to enjoy together, not to spend your time fighting over. If you're going to quarrel, we can just forget this pony idea completely.'

Jessica and Samantha quickly stopped arguing.

There was silence for a few minutes and then Jessica looked at her sister. 'Please, Samantha,' she said quietly, 'please can we get Sandy? You heard what Tina said yesterday – she's only six, she'll learn to jump better as she gets older. And I really, really like her.'

Samantha didn't say anything.

'We could have lessons on her, couldn't we, Dad?' Jessica asked.

Mr Parker nodded. 'Definitely – in fact, I think that would be a very good idea.'

'Then I guess she would improve, and she is pretty,' Samantha admitted. She frowned. 'OK, Jess, I'll think about it.'

Jessica exchanged hopeful looks with Lauren and they travelled the rest of the way in silence.

Lauren stared out of the window. She couldn't stop thinking about Michael. She wished she knew where he lived. If she did, she could call round with Twilight. Maybe they could fly back to Moonshine's field that night and see if he visited again.

When they arrived at the High Meadows farm, they saw that Tina was lunging Sandy in the training ring. The pony's golden coat gleamed in the sunlight and her thick, creamy-white tail floated out behind her. Her neck was arched and her dainty ears were pricked.

'Look, Sam!' Jessica exclaimed. 'Look how beautiful Sandy looks.'

Mr Parker stopped the car. Samantha, Jessica and Lauren jumped out and went over to the fence.

Seeing them, Tina waved. 'Hi, there,' she called, bringing the pony to a halt. 'Do you want to try Sandy and Bullfinch again?'

Jessica and Lauren looked at Samantha.

'Can we just try Sandy, please?' Samantha said to Tina.

⋆

Samantha and Jessica took it in turns to
ride Sandy. She was lively but obedient
and she jumped perfectly. By the time
they had finished, Samantha was smiling.

'I like her,' she said, riding the pony
over to the gate and halting her. 'She's
been much better today.'

'And she'll continue to improve,' Tina
said. 'You'll be able to do a lot with her.'

Jess turned to her dad. 'Can we have
her, Dad? Please!'

'If it's all right with Sam then, OK!'
Mr Parker smiled.

'Oh, thank you!' Jessica gasped. She
turned to Samantha. 'And thank you for
agreeing.'

'That's OK,' Samantha said happily. 'I really like her too, now I've ridden her again.'

While the girls put Sandy back in her stall, Mr Parker sorted out a price with Tina. It was arranged that she would deliver Sandy the next day.

'I can't believe she's going to be ours,' Jessica said as they got into the car.

'She's lovely,' Samantha said, looking genuinely pleased.

Mr Parker smiled. 'Well, I'm glad you two are in agreement at last. Come on, let's go home.'

As they turned out of the stables on to the quiet country road, something caught Lauren's eye. A boy with untidy dark hair

was riding a bike up and down the drive
of a nearby house. It was Michael! That
must be where he was staying with his
family!

She turned in her seat. Michael was
cycling in circles, looking bored.

'What are you looking at?' Jessica asked, following her gaze.

'Nothing,' Lauren said quickly.

To her relief, Jessica didn't press any more. She squeezed Lauren's arm. 'It's brilliant that Samantha and I are going to keep Sandy at Mel's, isn't it? We'll be able to ride together every day.'

'Yeah, it'll be great,' Lauren agreed. Mel Cassidy was one of their friends. She lived on the farm next door to Lauren but she was away at summer camp at the moment. Jessica started to talk about everything they would do together when Mel got back. Lauren listened vaguely but her thoughts were on Michael. Now she knew where he

lived maybe she could ride over on
Twilight to visit him. It wouldn't be that
far if they went through the woods
instead of going round by the roads.
Michael could have a ride on Twilight.
Determination filled Lauren. She was
going to help him. She was going to be
his friend.

It took Lauren and Twilight just over half
an hour to reach Michael's house through
the woods. A narrow track brought them
out on to the road beside his house.

As they rode along it, Lauren heard a
woman's voice coming from the garden.
'What would you like to do, Michael? We
could go swimming?'

There was no reply.

'Well, how about we go to the park?'
Lauren heard the woman say.

'Yeah, I guess,' Michael replied quietly.
Suddenly he spoke again. 'There's a pony!
I can hear a pony coming!'

He came running down the drive.
Recognizing Lauren, his eyes widened.

Lauren waved. 'Hi!'

'It's . . . it's you!' Michael stammered in
surprise.

Lauren grinned. 'Yes, and this is my
pony, Twilight. Do you like him?'

Michael nodded, looking astonished. 'I
didn't know you had a pony.'

'You left last night before I could tell
you,' Lauren explained.

'He looks just like Moonshine,'
Michael said.

Just then, a slim woman in her thirties
with short dark hair came down the
drive. She wore a pretty lilac sundress
with matching sandals. This must be
Jodie, Michael's foster mum. 'Who are
you talking to, Michael?' She stopped in
surprise when she saw Twilight and
Lauren.

'My name's Lauren Foster,' Lauren said
in her politest voice. 'I met Michael
yesterday –'

'When I went out for a walk,' Michael
put in quickly.

'I thought I'd call round and say hi,'
Lauren said. 'I hope you don't mind.'

'No, no, of course not,' Jodie said quickly.

'Michael told me he liked horses and I thought he might like a ride on my pony, Twilight,' Lauren said. 'We could ride in the woods.' She looked at Michael. 'If you bring your bike we could take it in turns to ride Twilight.'

Michael's face lit up. 'Great!' He turned to Jodie. 'I can, can't I?'

Jodie looked unsure. 'Well, are you sure you want to, honey?'

'Yes!' Michael exclaimed. 'Please can I?'

Jodie looked taken aback. 'Well, I guess so.' She glanced rather dubiously at Twilight. 'He is safe, isn't he?'

'Very,' Lauren said. 'And Michael can wear my hat.'

'Well, OK then,' Jodie said. 'But don't
be out too long.'

'Let's go into the woods,' Lauren said

as Michael pushed his bike down the drive to join her.

'This is fantastic!' Michael said, looking incredibly happy. 'How did you know where we were staying?'

Lauren explained about visiting the stables with Jessica's family. 'I saw you and thought I'd come round and visit.'

They reached the main trail. Lauren stopped Twilight and dismounted. 'Here, you have a go,' she said, handing her hat to Michael.

He put it on and mounted. 'Wow!' he said, beaming. 'It's amazing to be on a pony again.'

'You can trot and canter if you like,' Lauren said. 'Twilight's very good.'

To start with, Michael just walked, but as his confidence grew he trotted and cantered. He wasn't a very experienced rider, but his hands were light on the reins and he had very good balance. At last he reined Twilight in. His eyes were shining and his cheeks were flushed. 'That was brilliant! Twilight's fantastic, Lauren!'

Lauren smiled. 'I know. I'm really lucky.'

They rode for a while longer before Michael glanced at his watch. 'I guess I should be getting back.'

They headed to his house. Jodie was standing on the front porch looking out for them. 'There you are,' she said, coming down the steps towards them. 'I was starting to worry.'

Michael looked at the ground. 'Sorry,' he mumbled.

'It's OK,' Jodie said quickly. 'You must be hungry after your ride. Would you like some cookies? I baked them this morning.'

'Yes, please,' Lauren said.

Michael just nodded.

Lauren looked at him in surprise. He had been chatty out in the woods but now he was quiet. Jodie went inside.

'Your new mum seems really nice,' Lauren said in a low voice as she tied Twilight up to the fence at the side of the house.

'She is,' Michael said. There was a flatness in his voice. 'Both she and Chris are.' He sat down on the porch steps.

Lauren heard a note of reservation in his voice. 'But . . . ?' she asked, sitting down beside him.

For a moment Michael seemed to be wondering whether to say anything more. 'But they like different things from me,' he said, with a sigh. 'And that makes it hard.'

'What do you mean?' Lauren asked curiously.

'Well, Chris is really into baseball,' Michael replied, 'and he's always suggesting we go out and practise. And Jodie's always trying to get me to go swimming. I want to please them so I just go along with them, but really I just want to be with horses.'

'What do they say when you ask if you can go riding?' Lauren said.

Michael shrugged. 'I don't really ask. I did once or twice at the beginning but not any more.'

'Why not?' Lauren demanded in surprise.

'I want to make them happy,' Michael said softly. 'I want them to be glad they adopted me ...'

He broke off as Jodie came out of the house with a tray of drinks and chocolate-chip cookies.

'Here we are,' she said cheerfully,

putting the tray down on a table on the
porch. 'Have a cookie, Lauren.'

'Thank you,' Lauren said.

Jodie smiled. 'You know, I'm really pleased Michael's made a friend,' she said, sitting down on the steps too. 'What sort of things do you and your friends do in the holidays, Lauren?'

'We go to the creek and we go round to each other's houses, but most of all we ride,' Lauren said. 'Most of my friends have ponies.'

Jodie frowned. 'Really? Goodness. Things are different in the country. I grew up in the city. None of my friends ever rode.'

'Maybe Michael could start to ride while you're here,' Lauren suggested hopefully.

'Oh, I'm not sure,' Jodie said

doubtfully. 'You'd probably find it a bit boring, wouldn't you, Michael?'

'No!' Michael said, looking up quickly. 'I'd love to go riding.'

Lauren's eyes suddenly widened. She'd just had a brilliant idea!

CHAPTER
Five

'There are stables just round the corner from here,' Lauren burst out, looking at Jodie. 'Maybe Michael could help out there for the summer. He'd get to know people and he could be with horses.'

'That would be amazing!' Michael gasped. 'Can I?' he begged Jodie. 'Can I, please?'

Jodie raised her eyebrows. 'You wouldn't really want to, would you?'

'Yes,' Michael said. 'I'd love to.'

'Well, I suppose I *could* speak to the owner,' Jodie said.

Michael jumped up. 'Now?' he asked eagerly.

Jodie looked at him in amazement. 'You *are* keen. Well, OK. If it means that much to you then we can go and ask right away.' She finished her drink. 'I'll just lock the house and get my bag.'

Tina was leading Puzzle in from the field when Lauren arrived with Michael and Jodie. Jodie explained what they had come round for.

'Michael likes the idea of helping out,'
she said to Tina. 'Do you let children do
that?'

'Yes,' Tina replied. 'I usually have at
least five or six of them helping me in
exchange for rides. At the moment

several are away at camp. I could do with another pair of hands.' She looked at Michael. 'The trouble is, you're younger than most of my helpers and I won't be able to offer you many rides. I think a lot of the ponies will be too strong for you.'

'That's OK,' Michael said quickly. 'I'd be happy just to help.'

Twilight suddenly lifted his head and neighed. From the field by the car park came an answering whinny. Tina looked round. Moonshine was standing at the gate, staring at them.

She scratched her head. 'I suppose there's always Moonshine,' she said. 'She's very quiet. You could ride her, Michael.'

'I'd love to!' Michael said. He looked at Lauren, his eyes shining.

'OK then,' Tina said. 'It's settled. You come and help me with the yard chores and you can ride Moonshine in exchange.'

'And can I groom her and clean her tack?' Michael asked eagerly.

Tina smiled at his enthusiasm. 'As much as you like.'

Lauren was desperate to talk to Twilight about the good news. She couldn't wait until that evening and so on the way

home, she turned him down an
overgrown path that led to a hidden
glade in the woods.

Twilight walked forward eagerly,
pushing his way through the overhanging
branches. At last, the path opened out
into the sunny clearing. The grass was
springy and scattered with purple flowers.
Golden butterflies fluttered through the
warm, sweet-scented air. It was the most
secret place Lauren knew.

She said the Turning Spell.

'So, what do you think?' she asked, as
soon as the purple flash faded and
Twilight was standing in front of her in
his unicorn form.

'It's a wonderful idea,' Twilight said.

'Moonshine will love having someone to look after her each day.'

'And Michael will love helping with all the ponies,' Lauren said.

Twilight nodded. 'He would make a very good Unicorn Friend.'

'I know,' Lauren agreed. 'But I guess Moonshine's just going to have to wait for someone else to come along. Michael's only here for another five weeks, so he probably won't have time to find out that she's a unicorn.'

'Unless we help him,' Twilight said thoughtfully.

Lauren frowned. 'But we can't, Twilight. You know Unicorn Friends have to find out the truth about their

unicorn by themselves. That's why Mrs
Fontana could only hint that you were a
unicorn when I got you. We can't tell
Michael. If he's going to be a Unicorn
Friend, he has to believe in magic
enough to try the spell without knowing
whether it will work.'

Twilight nodded. 'I know, and I didn't
mean that we should tell him everything,
but couldn't we sort of *help* him find out
the truth?'

'I guess so,' Lauren said slowly. A
thought struck her. 'But if he does find
out, what will happen when he has to
leave Moonshine at the end of the
summer? It will be awful for him.'

'But isn't it better he has five weeks

as a Unicorn Friend than none?'
Twilight pointed out.

Lauren hesitated. She wasn't sure. It
was going to be hard enough for Michael
to leave Moonshine at the end of the
summer. Surely it would be a hundred
times worse if he had to leave her
knowing she was a unicorn?

'I don't know,' she said uncertainly. She
twisted her fingers in Twilight's mane and
wondered how she would feel if she had
to leave Twilight. *I couldn't bear it,* she
thought.

But what if she had never known
about his unicorn powers? Not known
what it was like to fly through the starry
skies, to feel the wind against her face

and Twilight's warm back beneath her?
Not even having the memories … No,
that would be even worse.

Twilight nuzzled her. 'What does your
heart say, Lauren?'

Lauren hesitated. Yes, it would be
dreadful for Michael to have to leave
Moonshine at the end of the summer
but, like Twilight had said, surely it was
better that he did that instead of never
knowing the truth. 'My heart says that we
should help him,' she said slowly.

'Well, I think that too,' Twilight said.
'So let's do it!'

Lauren looked at him. His dark eyes
were eager. She paused and then made a
decision.

'OK,' she agreed.

As she spoke, she felt a weight drop off her shoulders. She was sure that they were doing the right thing. They should help Michael. The only question was, *how were they going to do it*?

Even though Lauren thought about it all night, by the time she rode Twilight to Tina's the next morning she hadn't come up with an answer. Michael was riding Moonshine in the ring when she arrived. Moonshine was cantering eagerly, her ears pricked.

Michael saw them. 'Hi there,' he called.

'Moonshine's looking good,' Lauren said.

Michael bent down and hugged Moonshine's neck. 'She's brilliant.'

Tina came up the yard. Seeing Lauren, she smiled. 'Hello. Come to visit?'

Lauren nodded. 'You don't mind, do you?'

'Not at all,' Tina said. She looked at Michael. 'That's probably enough ring-work for Moonshine today. Why don't you go out into the woods for a short ride?'

'OK,' Michael said eagerly.

He rode out of the yard with Lauren. 'So, are you enjoying helping Tina?' she asked.

'It's brilliant,' Michael said, his face glowing. 'I've mucked out five stables

already this morning. This is going to be the best holiday ever.'

Lauren stroked Twilight. Michael's holiday would be even better if he knew about Moonshine. But how could she help him? She couldn't just start talking about unicorns out of the blue, he'd think she was crazy.

Beside her, Michael patted Moonshine's neck. 'You know, I'm sure Moonshine understands me when I talk to her,' he said. 'It's the way she looks at me. Like she's smarter than other ponies.' He laughed, sounding suddenly embarrassed. 'I guess that sounds really dumb.'

'No, it doesn't,' Lauren said. 'I know

what you mean. Twilight's the same. It's like they're different from other ponies.'

She glanced quickly at Michael. Maybe this was her chance to say something more. But what could she say? Before she could think of anything, Michael had pushed Moonshine on.

'Come on, let's canter!' he called.

Twilight jumped forward eagerly.

Lauren had no choice but to let him race after the little grey mare. She felt a wave of frustration at the wasted chance. Michael would be a perfect Unicorn Friend if only he would try the spell. But how did she get him to do that? Maybe if she had lots of time she could think of a way, but in just five weeks Michael would be going back to the city.

I'll come up with something, Lauren
thought, crouching low against Twilight's
neck as he cantered along the path. *I just
have to.*

CHAPTER
Six

A week passed by but Lauren didn't get any further in helping Michael work out Moonshine's secret. It was so frustrating. The more she saw him with Moonshine, and realized how much he loved the pony, the more she wanted him to be Moonshine's Unicorn Friend. But she just couldn't think of how to help him find out the truth. It just seemed impossible.

On Saturday, Michael came round to
her house and they went down to the
creek with Jessica and Samantha. They
took it in turns to ride Twilight and
Sandy. When they got back to her house
they brushed Twilight down and then
went up to Lauren's bedroom.

'I like your room,' Michael said,
looking admiringly at the horse posters
Lauren had stuck on the walls. He went
over to the window. 'Hey, you can see
Twilight's paddock from here.' Lauren's
unicorn book was lying open on the
window seat. Michael picked it up and
started to leaf through the pages. 'Wow!
This book looks interesting.'

Lauren's heart leapt. Of course! The

book had all the information Michael
needed.

Michael turned the first page. 'Look at

this pony! It looks just like Twilight and
Moonshine.'

'It's a picture of what unicorns look
like when they're disguised,' Lauren said.

'What do you mean?' Michael asked
looking round at her.

And suddenly Lauren knew as clearly
as anything what she had to do. 'Read the
book and it'll tell you,' she told him. 'You
can borrow it for the holidays.'

Michael looked surprised. 'Are you
sure?'

Lauren nodded. She loved the book
and didn't want to let it go — even for a
few weeks — but she was sure that it was
the only way that Michael was going to
learn about unicorns.

'OK, thanks,' he said, looking really pleased.

'Lauren!' Mrs Foster called up the stairs. 'Michael's mum is here.'

'We'd better go,' Lauren said. They went downstairs. Jodie was in the kitchen.

'Hi, honey,' she said, as Michael came in. 'Have you had a good day?'

Michael's eyes shone. 'It's been great! We rode to the creek with Lauren's friends, Jessica and Samantha, and we had a picnic and we swam.'

'That sounds fun,' Jodie said.

'It was fantastic!' Michael said. He looked round. 'I left my bag in your tack room, Lauren. Can I go and get it?'

'Sure,' Lauren said.

Michael put the unicorn book down on the table and ran outside. Jodie shook her head. 'I just can't believe the change in him since we moved out to the country for the summer,' she said to Mrs Foster. 'He used to be so quiet, but now he talks all the time – although only about horses.'

Mrs Foster laughed. 'That sounds very familiar. Is he going to carry on riding when you return to the city?'

'We'll see,' Jodie replied. 'Kids in the city don't really ride.'

Lauren looked at her mum. 'I used to ride lots when we lived in the city, didn't I, Mum?'

Mrs Foster nodded. 'We only moved here at Easter,' she explained to Jodie. 'Before then, Lauren used to ride every weekend. I know it's not so easy but there are riding schools and kids who ride. It's a good hobby, the children learn responsibility and have fun at the same time.'

Jodie looked surprised. 'Oh, I see.'

Michael came back in. 'I've got it,' he said, waving his bag. He started to put the book carefully inside. 'Thanks for having me round, Mrs Foster.'

'It's a pleasure,' Mrs Foster replied.

'What have you got there?' Jodie asked Michael, looking at the book.

'Lauren's lent it to me,' Michael

answered. 'It's a book about unicorns.'

Lauren sensed her mum glance quickly at her. Her mum knew that the unicorn book was one of the most precious things Lauren owned.

'Well, thank you very much, Lauren,' Jodie said.

'I'm sure Michael will take very good care of it.'

Lauren nodded and she and her mum saw Jodie and Michael to their car.

'So?' her mum said quietly to her as they waved them off.

'So?' Lauren said, but she knew what her mum was getting at.

'The book,' Mrs Foster said, looking at her. 'You love that book, Lauren. I'm surprised you're letting it out of your sight.'

'I know,' Lauren said. 'But Michael was looking at it today and he really liked it and ...' she hesitated, 'and I wanted to lend it to him for the summer.'

Her mum looked at her for a moment.

Then she smiled. 'There's a lot of good in you, Lauren Foster,' she said, hugging her. 'I'm proud you're my daughter.' She kissed Lauren's hair.

'Mum!' Lauren protested, but she felt a warm glow inside.

They walked back into the house.

'Michael really does love ponies, doesn't he?' Mrs Foster said. 'I guess it must be strange for his parents if they've never been into horses themselves and don't know anyone who rides. It probably seems an odd thing for him to want to do. Still, maybe if they see how much he enjoys himself this summer they'll let him carry on riding when they go home.'

Lauren nodded. But she couldn't really think about Michael going back to the city. Right now all that mattered was him finding out Moonshine's secret. Would he read the book? And, even more important, would he believe it? Lauren crossed her fingers. She and Twilight were just going to have to wait and see.

As Lauren rode Twilight over to High Meadows farm early the next morning, she said, 'I wonder if Michael read the book last night.' A thought struck her. 'What if he doesn't believe it? I had the book for ages before I tried turning you into a unicorn, Twilight.' She thought back to that time. 'It was only when I

saw the moonflowers in the secret glade
that I started to wonder if the spell might
actually work,' she said.

Twilight stopped dead.

'What's wrong?' Lauren said.

To her surprise, Twilight turned round
and started heading back down the track.
'What are you doing?' Lauren asked in
astonishment.

Twilight broke into a trot. Lauren
quickly loosened the reins. It was clear
he'd had an idea about something,
although she didn't know what. She let
him go where he wanted.

He trotted for about two minutes down
the path, finally halting by the overgrown
trail that led to the secret glade.

'Why have you stopped here?' Lauren said.

Twilight started to walk down the trail. Lauren ducked under the branches, wondering what he was doing. As soon as they entered the glade, he plunged his head down to the ground.

'You came here because you wanted to eat some grass?' Lauren said in surprise. Twilight stamped his hoof and she suddenly realized that he wasn't eating. He was nudging a moonflower with his nose.

Her eyes widened as she finally understood. 'You think we should take a moonflower to Michael?'

Twilight nodded.

'It's a brilliant idea!' Lauren said. 'He probably just thinks they're made-up flowers in the book, but if I give one to him he'll see that they really exist and maybe it'll make him try the spell.' She jumped off and picked a flower.

Twilight tossed his head as if to say, *That's what I thought all along.* Putting the flower in her pocket, Lauren remounted and they carried on their way.

Moonshine was tied up in the yard at High Meadows farm. Lauren noticed how much better she was looking. Her coat was now sleek and grey and her mane and tail were silky.

Michael came out of a barn with a

wheelbarrow. He was deep
in thought.

'Hi,' Lauren called.

Michael looked up. 'Oh ... hi.'

'Are you free to go for a ride?' Lauren
asked.

'I've got another two stalls to muck out first,' Michael said. 'But then I can.'

Lauren dismounted. 'I'll give you a hand.' She tied Twilight up by Moonshine and then set to work, watching Michael carefully all the time.

For a while Michael worked in silence, but at last he spoke. 'I was reading that book last night.'

Lauren glanced at him eagerly. 'What did you think?'

'It was really good.' He laughed in an embarrassed way. 'I mean, I know it's not true or anything but it's a really good story.'

Lauren remembered the flower. It was now or never. 'I brought you something

from the woods.' She took the
moonflower out of her jeans. The gold
spots on the tip of each purple petal
seemed to glow in the light of the stall.

Michael looked as if he was wondering
why she had brought him a flower but
then his eyes widened. 'It's a ... it's a ...'

'Moonflower,' Lauren murmured.

Michael's eyes flew to hers. 'They really exist?'

Lauren nodded. 'Yes, and so does the Twilight Star. It shines every night for ten minutes just after the sun sets.' She met his eyes. 'You just have to believe.'

Michael stared.

Fearing that, in a minute, she'd tell him everything, Lauren pushed the flower into his hand. 'Here, take it. I'll empty the wheelbarrow.' Before he could ask her any questions, she grabbed the handles of the wheelbarrow and pushed it out of the stall.

Michael didn't say much for the rest of the morning. He seemed to be thinking hard and even when they went out on a ride, he remained quiet. On the way home, Lauren caught him looking from Moonshine to Twilight. *Oh, please*, she thought, *try the spell tonight*.

They got back to the yard to find Jodie coming out of the office with Tina.

Seeing the surprise on Michael's face, Jodie smiled. 'Don't worry, nothing's wrong. I just thought I'd call round and see Tina and find out how you were doing.'

'And I said you were doing great,' Tina said. 'Moonshine's been like a different pony since you started looking after her, Michael.'

'So, this is Moonshine, is it?' Jodie asked, looking interested.

'Yes,' Michael answered. 'Isn't she perfect?'

Jodie stroked Moonshine. 'Oh, she is pretty.'

'She's the best,' Michael said, leaning forward and hugging the little grey pony. 'Aren't you, girl? She understands everything.'

Lauren patted Twilight's neck. If only Michael knew how true that was …

CHAPTER

Seven

The next morning, Lauren was up
and out of the house by nine
o'clock. She was longing to see Michael.

Michael was grooming Moonshine
when Lauren rode into the yard at High
Meadows farm. The little pony's coat
looked even glossier and her dark eyes
had a new sparkle.

'Hi,' Lauren called eagerly.

Michael swung round. 'Hello!' The
word almost burst out of him. He looked
very excited. 'Lauren!' he said, running
over. 'I've got to tell you something!
Something amazing about Moonshine.
She's a –'

'Ssshh,' Lauren interrupted, quickly
dismounting. 'I know.'

Michael stared at her. 'What do you
mean, you know?'

Lauren looked pointedly at Twilight.
He followed her gaze and his eyes
widened. 'Twilight's a –'

'You mustn't tell anyone,' Lauren broke
in. 'No one must know about him or
Moonshine. You can't talk about it – not
to anyone. It's got to be a secret.'

'But ... but ...' Michael stammered.

'Remember what the book said,'
Lauren reminded him.

They stared at each other for a
moment.

'I can't believe it's true,' Michael said,
shaking his head in wonder.

Lauren smiled. 'It is. Believe me, it is.'

Just then, Tina came out of the barn. She was showing a man and a dark-haired girl around the yard.

Lauren stiffened. 'I know that girl. She's called Monica Corder. She's in my class at school. What's she doing here?'

Michael looked surprised. 'She and her dad are looking for a pony, I think.'

'She's not very nice,' Lauren said.

'There's nothing here,' Monica was saying loudly to her dad. 'I want a pony that's going to win things.'

'Well, how about that chestnut with the blaze?' Mr Corder said. He turned to Tina. 'You said he'd won a lot lately.'

Monica folded her arms. 'But I don't want a chestnut, I want a grey.'

'Why don't you just give him a try, Monica?' Mr Corder said.

'I guess I could,' Monica said grudgingly.

'Michael,' Tina called. 'Can you tack up Puzzle for me, please?'

Monica glanced in their direction. Seeing Lauren, she frowned in surprise. 'Lauren! What are you doing here?' she said, speaking as if Lauren had no right to be in Tina's yard. Before Lauren could reply, Monica's eyes had fallen on Moonshine. 'Hey! What's *that* pony's name?' she demanded.

'Moonshine,' Michael replied.

Monica's green gaze swept over Moonshine's soft grey coat and silky mane and tail. 'I like her,' she declared. She turned to her father. 'Dad! I like this pony. She's really pretty. I'll try her too.'

Lauren and Michael stared at each other in horror.

Mr Corder turned to Tina. 'We'll have that one saddled up too, please.'

'Well, actually,' Tina said, stepping forward, 'I've already got someone booked to see that pony later this morning. They've asked to be given first refusal on her – that means they have first choice on whether to buy her or not,' she explained to Monica. 'So although you can try her out, I have to wait and let the other people see her as well.'

Lauren stared at Tina. There were other people who wanted Moonshine? But they couldn't. Moonshine couldn't be sold! Especially not now Michael had discovered her secret.

Monica scowled. 'But I like her best.'

'I'm sorry, but that's the situation,' Tina said.

'Well, I'll try her anyway,' Monica said.

Tina turned to Michael. 'Can you tack Moonshine up as well, please, Michael?'

Michael looked totally shocked as he fetched the tack. Lauren felt awful. Poor Michael. What would he do if Moonshine was sold?

★

Monica mounted Moonshine. She landed
with a thump in the saddle and
Moonshine took a surprised step
backwards.

'Walk on!' Monica said sharply, digging
her heels into Moonshine's sides. When

Moonshine didn't respond immediately, Monica smacked her with her riding crop. Moonshine jumped forward in alarm. Lauren glanced at Michael. His face was pale.

'Just give her time to get used to you, Monica,' Tina called, standing by the gate with Puzzle.

Monica dug her heels in again. 'Come on.'

Moonshine's walk slowed down. Monica smacked her again with her crop. 'Walk on!'

But Moonshine just got slower and slower. Although she was very good for Michael she seemed determined to be as lazy as possible for Monica.

After a circuit of the ring, Monica stopped Moonshine by the gate. 'She's a useless pony,' she said scathingly. 'She's so slow.' She dismounted. 'She's way too lazy for me.'

Lauren felt a rush of relief.

'Oh well, never mind,' Tina said cheerfully. 'I think the people who are coming later this morning will be just perfect for her.'

Lauren glanced at her. Tina didn't sound like she cared about Michael's feelings. Surely she knew how upset he was at the thought of Moonshine being sold?

'I'll try the other pony instead,' Monica said.

As she mounted Puzzle, Tina turned to Michael. 'Seeing as Moonshine's tacked up, why don't you take her out for a quick ride in the woods, Michael? The other people won't be here for a while and you can smarten her up when you get back.'

Michael nodded. Lauren realized that Tina had suggested the ride to be kind because she could see that Michael was only just managing to fight back his tears.

As they rode out of the yard, Lauren looked at him. 'I'm really sorry,' she said.

Michael stared at Moonshine's mane. 'She can't be sold,' he said in a low trembling voice.

'At least Monica didn't want her,'

Lauren said, trying to cheer him up. 'And maybe she'll be just as lazy for these other people, then they won't want her either.' She leaned forward. 'Moonshine. You've got to do exactly what you did with Monica this afternoon. These people *mustn't* buy you.'

Moonshine nodded slightly.

'And maybe we can put these people off her,' Lauren said, trying to think of something. 'Tell them that she's naughty or something.'

'Yes.' Michael looked suddenly hopeful, but then his face fell. 'I won't be here. Jodie and Chris are taking me shopping later.'

'Well, I'll stay,' Lauren said. 'I'll try and

think of something.'

Michael swallowed. 'I know I've got to say to goodbye to Moonshine at the end of the summer but not now, especially not after finding out that she's a –'

'Ssshh!' Lauren said quickly in case there was anyone nearby in the woods who might overhear.

She saw a tear fall down Michael's face. 'I'll think of something,' she said desperately. 'I promise.'

CHAPTER

Eight

As Lauren and Michael rode back to the yard, Tina came out of a barn. 'Great, you're back. Can you brush Moonshine over and oil her hooves, Michael?'

'Did Monica buy Puzzle?' Lauren asked.

Tina shook her head. 'She didn't like him, although at least he was better behaved than Moonshine.' She walked over and patted the little grey pony next to Michael. 'I've never known you so lazy, girl. I guess you just didn't like her.'

Leaving Michael to smarten up Moonshine, Tina went to the tack room. Lauren tried desperately to think of a plan.

'I'm going to have to go in a minute,' Michael said, looking at his watch after he'd oiled Moonshine's hooves. 'Have you thought of anything, Lauren?'

She shook her head. 'Not yet.'

'What am I going to do?' he said.

Just then there was the sound of a car coming down the drive. Tina came out of the tack room. 'Ah, here are the people to see Moonshine.'

Michael and Lauren looked round at the black car.

'No it's not, Tina. It's my mum and dad,' Michael said. 'They must have decided to come and get me. We're going shopping.'

'Yes,' Tina said with a smile. 'I know.'

Lauren looked at her. There was some-thing about the way she was smiling . . .

Michael had obviously noticed it too. He looked from Tina to his mum and dad who were parking the car. 'What . . . what's going on?' he asked.

'Yes, you're going shopping, Michael – for a pony,' Tina told him.

Both Lauren and Michael stared at her.

'A pony!' Michael gasped.

Tina nodded. 'When your mum came
to see me yesterday, it was to talk about
buying you Moonshine. I suggested she
come with your dad to see her today.'

'I . . . I don't believe it,'
Michael stammered. Jodie
and Chris got out of the car.
Jodie small and slim, Chris tall and skinny
with round glasses. Michael raced over to
them. 'I'm getting a pony? I'm really
getting Moonshine?' His eyes looked
almost wild.

'If you want her,' Jodie said.

'Oh yes, I do! More than anything!' Michael cried.

'Then she's yours,' Chris smiled.

'But where will I keep her?' Michael burst out.

'I phoned some stables in the city and found one near home,' Jodie said. 'They have a pony club there. You'll be able to learn all sorts of things – have lessons, go in shows.'

Chris nodded. 'And they run stable management classes for the parents too, so Jodie and I will be able to learn about horses and help you.' He squeezed Michael's shoulder. 'If you want us to, of course.'

Michael looked almost lost for words.

'That ... that would be great.' He swung round. 'Lauren! Did you hear that?'

She grinned at him. 'Yes. It's great!'

Michael grabbed hold of Jodie and Chris's hands. 'Come and see Moonshine,' he said, half pulling them up the yard.

Moonshine whickered as they got close. Michael ran over and patted her proudly. 'You're going to be mine!' he told her.

'We just want you to be happy,' Jodie said to him, smiling at his joyful face. 'It's all we've ever wanted. We only tried to get you to do things like baseball and swimming because we thought you'd enjoy them.'

'I know,' Michael said. 'It's just that I like horses.'

'I guess we only realized that once we saw how much you've liked coming and helping here,' Chris said. 'I mean before that you'd only mentioned riding once or twice.'

'I know.' Michael looked awkward. 'It was because you didn't seem keen on the idea when I did mention it so I stopped. I wanted to please you and do what you wanted.'

'I think we've all been trying a bit too hard,' Jodie said. 'Maybe now the three of us can really start being a family.' She walked forward and patted the little grey pony. 'Sorry, I should have said the four

of us, of course. Welcome to the family,
Moonshine.'

Moonshine whickered softly and
Michael threw his arms round Jodie and
Chris in delight. They
hugged him
tightly.

Lauren's thoughts were whirling. She could hardly believe that after she and Michael had been so worried things had all ended perfectly.

Michael sighed happily and looked at Moonshine. 'You're going to be mine, Moonshine! I can't believe it!'

Tina smiled at him. 'I told you she'd be going to a perfect home, didn't I?'

Michael nodded. 'But I didn't know you meant me. I'm so lucky. She's the best pony in the world!'

Twilight snorted.

'One of the two best ponies in the world,' Michael corrected himself.

The adults laughed.

'Everyone thinks their pony is the best

pony in the world,' Tina commented.

Michael grinned at Lauren. 'But in our case it's true, isn't it?'

Lauren grinned back. 'Definitely,' she said.

The night air was warm and still as Lauren and Twilight stood in the shadow of the trees waiting for Michael to visit Moonshine. Twilight bent to rub his head against his knee as a shaft of moonlight shone down through the branches and glanced off his pearly horn.

'He's coming,' Lauren whispered. 'Look.'

Twilight lifted his head. Michael was hurrying down the drive.

Moonshine was waiting by the gate.
She whinnied softly, her ears pricked.
Michael climbed the gate and stood
beside her, his hand on her grey neck.

Lauren saw his lips move. Suddenly there
was a bright purple flash and Moonshine
was transformed into a unicorn. She was
beautiful, her long tail swept almost to

the ground and her coat gleamed like mother of pearl in the moonlight.

'What should we do?' Twilight murmured. 'Do you think we should go over and say hello?'

Lauren looked at Michael and Moonshine. They were standing only inches apart, their heads almost touching. They looked lost in their own little world.

'No,' Lauren said suddenly. 'Let's leave them.'

As she spoke, Michael got on to Moonshine's back. Moonshine turned and, pushing off with her hind legs, she cantered up into the sky. Lauren smiled, her eyes shining. At long last Moonshine

had found a true Unicorn Friend and it
wasn't just for the summer. It looked like
they were going to be together for a

long, long time to come – just like her and Twilight.

As she turned Twilight for home, Lauren buried her face in his silvery mane. They had so many more wonderful adventures ahead of them – she couldn't wait!

Do you love magic, unicorns and fairies?

Join the sparkling

My
Secret
Unicorn

fan club today!

It's FREE!

You will receive a sparkle pack, including:

Stickers   **Badge**
Membership card   **Glittery pencil**

Plus four Linda Chapman newsletters every year,
packed full of fun, games, news and competitions.
And look out for a special card on your birthday!

How to join:

Visit mysecretunicorn.co.uk and enter your details

Send your name, address, date of birth* and email address (if you have one) to:

Linda Chapman Fan Club, Puffin Marketing,
80 Strand, London, WC2R 0RL

Your details will be kept by Puffin only for the purpose of sending information regarding Linda Chapman
and other relevant Puffin books. It will not be passed on to any third parties.
You will receive your free introductory pack within 28 days

*If you are under 13, you must get permission from a parent or guardian

Notice to parent/guardian of children under 13 years old: Please add the following to their email/letter including
your name and signature: I consent to my child/ward submitting his/her personal details as above.

My Secret Unicorn

When Lauren recites a secret spell, Twilight turns into a beautiful unicorn with magical powers! Together Lauren and Twilight learn how to use their magic to help their friends.

Look out for more *My Secret Unicorn* adventures:

The Magic spell,
Dreams Come True, Flying High,
Starlight Surprise, Stronger Than Magic,
A Special Friend, A Winter Wish, A Touch of Magic,
Snowy Dreams, Twilight Magic

Have you read them all?

Puffin by Post

My Secret Unicorn